p 8. Onthiological discernment w/
    NSSic: Basic, etc.

p 5 The Bible & Evangelical Theology.

p 33 either/or — Barth: not
                    evangelical.

p 23, 24 on the advent of Hitler.

p 40-41 what it means to be a Xtian

A
Karl Barth
Reader

Luther — Barth   one is not a Xtian
but continually becoming a Xtian.

A
Karl Barth
Reader

edited by
ROLF JOACHIM ERLER
and
REINER MARQUARD

Edited and Translated
by
GEOFFREY W. BROMILEY

Grand Rapids
William B. Eerdmans Publishing Company

Copyright © 1986 by William B. Eerdmans Publishing Company
255 Jefferson Ave. S.E., Grand Rapids, Mich. 49503

Translation of *Mit dem Anfang anfangen: Karl Barth-Lesebuch*
© 1985 Theologischer Verlag Zürich

Library of Congress Cataloging-in-Publication Data

Barth, Karl, 1886-1968.
A Karl Barth reader.

Translation of: Mit dem Anfang anfangen.
Includes indexes.
1. Theology.   I. Erler, Rolf Joachim.   II. Marquard,
Reiner.   III. Bromiley, Geoffrey W.   IV. Title.
BT80.B3613   1985   230'.044   86-6287

ISBN 0-8028-0190-0

Contents

To Max Zellweger-Barth
and
Hinrich Stoevesandt
with thanks

Translator's Preface

Prepared for the Barth centennial, this selection from Barth's works serves admirably as an introduction to his thinking for those who have neither the time nor perhaps the desire to plunge into his bulky output for themselves. Indeed, since it draws on various writings that are not readily available, if at all, in English, it may be a useful supplement where some knowledge of Barth and his theology already exists. The translation follows the Swiss original closely except for some shortening of the introductions and chronology, and a few minor excisions in longer passages, to reduce the size and cost. I have used available translations where possible, but sometimes, especially in the case of older or less accessible texts, I have made new renderings. Readers who wish to consult the English passages in detail will welcome the addition of the English page numbers and also of an index of English translations.

Pasadena, Advent 1985   **Geoffrey W. Bromiley**

Introduction

In a sermon on Psalm 111:10, Barth put the question: "What is wisdom?" and answered that it is knowing about life or the art of living. These arise from being able to live, and this is the greatest knowledge and the most difficult art. All of his life Karl Barth tried constantly to start afresh in the fear of the Lord that is the beginning of wisdom, and he would freely admit that he was only a child who had grasped, understood, and perceived nothing at all. With astonishment and wonder, he did not seek or desire much, but only the one thing with which he finally thought he had found all things (*Predigten 1954–1967*, Zurich [1981], pp. 120–129). We have all things when we are content with God's grace (I), not defiantly and helplessly grasping at truth as a religious position that we ourselves choose (II). For we have then seen that the decision has been made once for all for us in Jesus Christ (III). Because of this decision we have the gift of freedom, to which we may respond freely and gratefully, renouncing all unfree ideologies and principles (IV). Freed by Christ, we do not sleep in life's different situations but keep our senses alert simply to hear and proclaim God's Word as though nothing had happened (V). As we are taken up and hidden in this Word, no suffering is suffering without Christ, but with him, and affliction thus loses its sting in a relaxed confidence (VI). We rely on his having overcome evil and thus avoid the frenzy of self-exaltation and ungodliness (VII). Content with him, we may laugh and weep, we grow in wisdom, we ask and pray and sigh and cry like children to their heavenly Father, and we are grateful that we may always begin again at the beginning (VIII).

The chapter headings point to typical thought forms in Barth's theology. The selections from various genres cover all Barth's active life. They are usually set up chronologically in each chapter. Our main aim has been not to show changes in Barth's theology but to document his increasing focus on Christ as the one and final word. The brief introductions are partly formal, partly material, and the references come at the end of the extracts. The primer is for both students and non-students, and on Barth's centenary the work is designed to let Barth himself speak to us from the wealth of his writings, in which we may learn to know him as a Christian, a theologian, and a fellow man.

August 1985   Rolf Joachim Erler and Reiner Marquard

Prologue

ON OCTOBER 29, 1944, BARTH *preached in Basel Minster on Lamentations 3:21–23, with an eye on his own "limit," and with some reference to the centenary of Nietzsche's birth.*

All of us, however great, significant, or good, have a definite circle of life, a space, a time, a force, and opportunities, but also a limit that we cannot cross. In the long run and at root, beyond that limit none of us can be understood or valued or alive for others. Sometimes, on a hundredth birthday, we may be rediscovered and people may look at us and read something about us, but a fortnight later they will no longer speak about people who are long since gone.

Mark you, this is always the case. Our interests and relationships — and happily too the misunderstandings and troubles under which we live — will necessarily come up against a point in this life when they will no longer signify. We will have to give up what we have desired, pull down what we have built, and let our achievements be surpassed and supplanted by those of others.

It would be good for us, and would help us, if we could keep this in view. We have not always done so. When things are present, we do not usually think of them ending. Everything seems unending: friends, concerns, projects, failures, possessions, desires, good aims — so infinitely good! — and evil passions. We ourselves, and our fellows, and what we value about them, and even more so their faults! Alas, we have to realize how terrible this is. The unending is our enemy. Un-

1

ending things get on top of us; they possess us instead of our possessing them. We become prisoners of life instead of being free. We should recall that in truth all things have an end. It is so. In this light we cannot live indifferently. We laugh and weep and are cross and love and take life seriously, but humanly so, not superhumanly or in animal fashion. An animal seriousness seems very lofty and fine, but we suffer from nothing more in life than from this seriousness that will not think of the end. How good it would be for us, and how it would help us, if we could take it to heart that all things have an end, and if for this very reason we could hope.

Fürchte dich nicht! Predigten aus den Jahren 1934 bis 1948, Munich (1949), pp. 278f.

I. The Theological Axiom

"Thy grace is sufficient for me."

*B*EGINNING *IS HARD, and Karl Barth found it so. He did not begin with himself and build a refuge for himself on his own possibilities. He had in mind a beginning in which he would more resolutely and relevantly than before let the Bible itself speak normatively in our thinking and preaching* (Offene Briefe 1945–1968, p. 191). *For Barth this strictly meant beginning afresh with God, with the death and resurrection of Jesus Christ, and with the free mercy revealed and at work in him (p. 52). The saying in 2 Corinthians 12:9, "My grace is sufficient for thee," formed a summary of this message and was in some sense his decisive theological axiom. As theologians—and nontheologians—we cannot begin on our own or in our own name. Hence the only possibility in theological work is to recall that all-sufficient grace and to strive against forgetting that Jesus Christ is the author and finisher of faith (Heb. 12:2). Barth preached on 2 Corinthians 12:9 in Basel prison on Dec. 31, 1962. He preached there twenty-eight times between 1954 and 1964, usually on brief texts.*

"My grace is sufficient for thee" (2 Cor. 12:9). This is a very short text—a mere six words—the shortest I have ever preached on. The brevity is an advantage for you; you can retain it better. I might say in passing that every time I come here I am very concerned that not so much my sermon but the text that it follows may really sink in and go with you. This time then: "My grace is sufficient for thee." The wonderful spice of this saying lies in its brevity. The six words are enough. Some of you may have heard that in the last forty years I have written many books, some large. I will freely and frankly and gladly admit that these six words say much more and much better things than all the heaps of paper with which I have surrounded myself. They are enough – which cannot be said even remotely of my books. What may be good in my books can be at most that from afar they point to what these six words say. And when my books are long since outdated and forgotten, and every book in the world with them, these words will still shine with everlasting fullness: "My grace is sufficient for thee."

Predigten 1954–1967, Zurich (1981), p. 220.

Barth gave his last course at Basel in the winter semester 1961–62. In it he tried to give an account of what he had "basically sought, learned, and represented" (Foreword to Evangelical Theology).

Theological work is distinguished from other kinds of work by the fact that anyone who desires to do this work cannot proceed by building with complete confidence on the foundation of questions that are already settled, results that are already achieved, or conclusions that are already arrived at. He cannot continue to build today in any way on foundations that were laid yesterday by himself, and he cannot live today in any way on the interest from a capital amassed yesterday. His only possible procedure every day, in fact every hour, is to begin anew at the beginning. . . . Yesterday's memories can be comforting and encouraging for such work only if they are identical with the recollection that this work, even yesterday, had to begin at the beginning and, it is to be hoped, actually began there. In theological science, continuation always means "beginning once again at the beginning."

Einführung in die evangelische Theologie, Zurich (1985), pp. 181f. (ET *Evangelical Theology,* Grand Rapids [1979] p. 165).

On February 6, 1917, Barth spoke at Leutwil on "The New World in the Bible." With the Leutwil pastor, Eduard Thurneysen, he was then engaged in a new study of the Bible, especially Romans.

If we come to the Bible with our own questions—How are we to think about God and the world? How do we reach the divine? What about ourselves?—it gives us the answer: Dear people, this is all your own affair, you must not ask me! Is it better to hear mass or a sermon? Does the Salvation Army have true Christianity, or does Christian Science? Has old paster Müller a true faith, or has young pastor Meyer? Should religion be more a matter of understanding, will, or feeling?—you can and must settle all these things for yourselves. If you will not take up my questions, then you may find in me all kinds of arguments and counterarguments regarding this or that position; but you will never get at the heart of things that way. The only possible result will be a high degree of human correctness that is very far from what is really true and what ought to be true in our lives. Note this: Human thoughts about God do not constitute the content of the Bible; rather, it is the true divine thought about humanity. The Bible does not tell us how we should speak about God but what God says to us, not how we may find the way to him but how he has sought and found the way to us, not what is the proper relation in which we must stand to him but what is the covenant that he has made with all who in faith are the children of Abraham, and that he has sealed once and for all in Jesus Christ. This is what stands in the Bible.

Das Wort Gottes und die Theologie, Munich (1929), pp. 27f. (ET *The Word of God and the Word of Man*, New York [1957], cf. pp. 42f.).

For Easter 1927, Barth wrote an article entitled "Resurrection," which came out in the Münchner Neueste Nachrichten *on April 16, 1927.*

The situation regarding the preaching and accepting of the basic Christian term *resurrection* is this. If the church speaks about it aright, it does so with startled humility, to which the entrusted revelation that it must proclaim, however old and familiar, will always be new, and just as transcendent and inconceivable as it was the first day. And if the world hears the term aright, it will do so with the joy of discovery or with a sharp protest, as at something unheard of. If the word really bursts on the scene, it poses for both church and world the need to begin afresh in its understanding of Christian truth. If it has become small change—pronounced and received as self-evident, already understood, a plausible concept whose meaning is at the disposal of speaker and hearer as a known factor—then no matter how piously and profoundly the game is played, it is a false game. When seriously spoken, this word is full of distances. With the answer to life that it alone will give in each age as though it were never spoken or heard before, it questions afresh all the answers that the world and the church have found, everywhere pointing away from the truth that we can and should tell ourselves to the truth that we can only be told, everywhere demanding a decision between faith and unbelief, between obedience and disobedience, a decision that must be taken today. If we cannot see these distances and do not come into this crisis, we may speak and hear well without even having to begin to understand, but this will be an infallible symptom that the basic Christian word "resurrection" is not on the scene but some fine equivalent of a different origin and meaning. All Christian words have such innocuous but fatal alter egos, not least the word "God," for which at Easter the word "resurrection" is a pregnant substitute. The church and the world have good reason not to be deceived—nor to let themselves be deceived—in this regard.

Zwischen den Zeiten 5, Munich [1927], pp. 201f.

On March 10, 1933, a few days after the Reichstag fire, Barth gave a lecture in Copenhagen on "The First Commandment as a Theological Axiom."

Theology is an attempt by means of human thought and speech to achieve scientific clarity on the question of the church's basis, law, and proclamation. From the very first, then, it stands in the sphere of Scripture and the first commandment. Where axioms stand in other sciences, in theology—before all theological thought or speech—there stands at the source or root, basic and critical, though in a way different from that of other axioms, the command: "Thou shalt have no other gods but me" (Ex. 20:3). Theologically, I think and speak responsibly when in my thinking and speaking I know that I am responsible to this command, and when I see in this responsibility the accountability to a court from which there can be no appeal because it is the last and supreme court and absolutely decisive. "Thou shalt have no other gods but me." Nothing is less self-evident than that theology should have no other gods alongside the God of the church. It is as little self-evident today as it was at Sinai, or on the morning that Jesus Christ rose from the dead, that this God rises up and makes himself heard—"I am the Lord thy God"—and makes other gods as nothing, and takes our hearts captive so that we have to fear *him* and love *him* and trust *him*. Theology too, and it precisely, is always questioned where its heart and concerns and interests really lie, and whether its heart is secretly divided between this God and other gods. . . . It is asked where it really comes from and where it is really going. . . . The battle against natural theology, which is unavoidable in the light of the first commandment as a theological axiom, is the battle for true obedience in theology. . . . Every theology has other gods, especially where it least perceives them. . . . Even the theology that is most strictly oriented to the first commandment has every reason to be open to an objection that might be raised against it in terms of this commandment. It too is never justified by its work but only, if at all, by the forgiveness of sins. Hence

the battle in theology . . . can be fought only with penulti-
mate and not with absolute seriousness and anger. We know
no theology of which we can say with final definiteness that
it does have other gods as well as the God of the church. We
can only remember together the first commandment. We can
only ask, only protest, when the clarity of the relation of theology to the first commandment again seems to be threatened. But when we have said all that needs to be said, the
"bond of peace" (Eph. 4:3) must come to light again, an
awareness of the superior wisdom of the Lord of the church,
the promise: "Lo, I am with you always" (Mt. 28:20), which,
applying to ourselves, we can apply no less to others. Only
in common hope can we properly wage the necessary theological battle.

Theologische Fragen und Antworten, Zurich (1957), pp. 135f., 142f.

*At the invitation of the Protestant Theological Faculty, Barth gave
three lectures in Paris, April 10–12, 1934, the third on the subject
"Theology."*

Of all the sciences theology is the most beautiful, the one
that moves both heart and mind most richly, the closest to
human reality, the one that gives the clearest view of the
truth that all sciences investigate. . . . How poor are those
theologians and that theology that have not yet seen this! But
of all the sciences theology is also the most difficult and dangerous, the one that might lead most easily to despair, or,
which is worse, to arrogance; the one that, dissipating or os-
sifying, might become the worst caricature of itself. Can any
science become so monstrous or tedious as theology? Those
are not theologians who are not startled by its abysses or who
have ceased to be so. . . . Theology is not a private reserve
of theologians. It is not a private affair for professors. Happily, there have always been pastors who have understood it
better than most professors. Nor is it a private affair for pas-

tors. Happily, there have always been church members and many congregations who have discharged its function quietly but vigorously while their pastors were theological babes or barbarians. Theology is a matter for the church. It does not get on well without professors and pastors. But its problem, the purity of the church's service, is put to the whole church. There are in principle no nontheologians in the church. The term "laity" is one of the worst in the vocabulary of religion and ought to be banished from Christian conversation. Those who are not professors or pastors share responsibility if the theology of their professors and pastors is to be good and not bad. And because revelation, or the church in its nature and purpose, is a human affair, we now say very generally that theology too is a human affair. There are times that need theology so urgently that one might say that, no matter how few may realize it, it is *the* human affair.

Theologische Fragen und Antworten, Zurich (1957), pp. 175, 183f.

On March 22, 1940 (Good Friday), Barth gave a radio address on the new orientation in Protestant theology.

The Bible speaks only when we let it speak the first word, when we let it posit a new beginning in our thoughts. . . . What we were not told at university and now had to learn for ourselves is that the freedom of Christian thought consists of obedience. Simple though this sounds, it signified then — and still signifies if we keep in view its implications — a Copernican revolution to realize it.

The idea that, in competition with the school or socialism or other altruistic institutions and efforts, the church has to serve the general improvement of the world and humanity can no longer be held on a biblical basis. It ought to be clear to us that the church is the place where Jesus Christ, his cross and resurrection, his humility and lordship, may and must be proclaimed. That means that it is the place where God speaks to us as the one before whom we are all lost, even though all our attempts at betterment are most successful, even though we are the cleverest and purest people in the best social order. We are all lost because before him we are always sinners; but he still invites us to cling to him, and he will be a comfort and admonition and promise for all of us just as we are. *We do not build his kingdom nor procure our own salvation.* He himself does both by giving us his word and awakening faith. For us there remains only the immeasurable thing of being thankful to him all our lives and with all our lives. This is what we found in the Bible when we began to let it speak to us quietly and without prejudgment. Clearly, we now had to make it the content of our preaching and teaching. It was also clear to us that, for all our respect for other callings, we could no longer play with the idea of being secretaries or teachers or journalists or politicians. It was also clear that theology as the presupposition of the church's work, biblical study, the task of understanding the church's past, and the systematic question of the content of Christian faith (what one calls dogmatics) now had to take on new significance for us. It was clear that the church needs theology, for if its task is to hear and proclaim God's word, it cannot easily test itself too much. It was clear as well that theology needs the church, the church that should hear and proclaim God's word.

Kirchenblatt für die reformierte Schweiz 96, Basel (1940), p. 99.

Barth lectured on "Protestant Theology in the 19th Century" in Münster (1926 and 1929–30) and then again in Bonn (1932–33). The lectures were published in 1947. In his foreword Barth says that we should love as well as criticize our predecessors.

The subject matter, theology, is methodological, critical reflection on the presupposition of the church's office as witness. Servants of God's Word have to be theologians because they have to bear witness to God's Word by what they say in preaching, teaching, and pastoral care. Not God's Word itself, but their service of it, the specific service of their witness in their own words, is conditioned by human investigation and needs methodological, critical reflection. The issue is always that of a hearing that has to precede speaking, the hearing in any given present of the Word of God that is documented in the Bible. Because each present is different, theology cannot be merely a confirmation and imparting of the results already achieved by some classical period. Hence the reflection always has to be new. Theological work always has to be done in all seriousness from the very beginning. When it is done thus, the theology of past ages, both classical and less classical, will also speak and be heard; for we are present with it in the sphere of the church. Being in the sphere of the church, we are not in a vacuum. The required beginning at the beginning cannot mean beginning on our own. The communion of saints is relevant here—mutual bearing and being borne, questioning and being questioned, sharing responsibility as sinners gathered together in Christ. Regarding theology, we cannot be in the church without being responsible to past as well as present theology. Augustine, Thomas, Luther, Schleiermacher, and all the rest are alive, not dead. They still speak and seek to be heard as living voices, as surely as we know that we are in the church, and they with us. In their day, discharging the same task, they contributed the same reflection that is required of us. As we engage in it, they speak to us through their contribution, and we cannot do it today without letting them speak too; for we are responsible not only to God, to ourselves, to people of our own age, and to our theological contemporaries, but also to them. There is no past in the church, nor in theology: "All live to Him." Only heretics, indeed arch-heretics, those who are lost to God's invisible church, belong to the past. But we are in no position to establish such arch-heresy, not even among pagans, much less Jews or suspect, perhaps very suspect, Christians. There are only relative heretics, and even though we see and judge their acknowledged folly and wickedness, we can and should let them speak in theology. In any age, theology must be strong enough and free enough to listen quietly, attentively, and openly to the voices not merely of the classical past but of all the past. God is the Lord of the church; he is the Lord of theology too. We cannot anticipate which co-workers of the past will be welcome in our own work, and which not. It may always be that those unexpected and even unwelcome voices will be the ones we particularly need in some sense.

Die protestantische Theologie im 19. Jahrhundert, Zurich (1985), pp. 2f. (ET Valley Forge [1973], cf. pp. 16f.).

On September 21, 1953, in Bielefeld, Barth gave an address to the Society for Evangelical Theology on the theme "The Gift of Freedom." As the basis of an evangelical ethics, he discussed the ethos of the free theologian.

Much theology that is undertaken and executed with great zeal, piety, learning, and perspicacity, lacks the light and serenity without which theologians are gloomy guests on this dark earth and uninspiring teachers of their brethren. . . . If we will not begin with God, as thoughtful people we can begin only with ourselves and our own misery, with the nothingness that threatens us and the world, with no more than cares and problems. And there after a short time we shall also end. . . . We can have what we lack—including materially—only if we execute a *turn*. None of us have this turn wholly behind us, for we can execute it only when we are given the freedom to do so, in the event of obedience. Each morning, then, and perhaps each hour, we must execute it as we face each new theological task. And we must not complain that it is impossible for this reason. It is not, of course, a dialectical trick that we can learn and need only repeat with ease. Without calling on God—"Our Father, who art in heaven" (Mt. 6:9)—we cannot execute it. We have to realize that fundamentally theology is worship, thanksgiving, and petition, a liturgical action. The ancient saying that the law of praying is the law of believing is not just a pious saw but one of the cleverest things ever said about the method of theology. At any rate, we can do nothing without that turn. Free and proper theological thinkers live by it. In the invocation, thanksgiving, and petition in which it is possible, they may pursue free thinking as the children of God.

Free theologians, then, begin comfortably and cheerfully with the Bible, not because they are dyed with some orthodoxy old or new, not because they must . . . but because they have the gift and permission to do so; not because they do not read and value other books, both spiritual and secular, both serious and stimulating (let us not forget the newspaper), but because they hear in the Bible the witness to the free God and free people, and because as students of the Bible they may themselves become witnesses to divine and human freedom. It is not a matter of some doctrine of the canon and inspiration of Holy Scripture but of the practice, not without inspiration, of a certain way of dealing with canonical Scripture. This has spoken to them and still does. They hear it. They study it. They do so analytically, historically, and critically so as to hear it better. But as free theologians they cannot start with this analysis, with the so-called assured results of historical, critical research, with what are called exegetical findings. This is not just because these usually change every thirty years and from one exegete to another, and therefore cannot provide any certain starting point, but because the analytical study of the Bible or any other text, although it is a necessary condition of hearing what it says, cannot as such guarantee or include this hearing. Hearing comes with synthetic reading and study. Free theologians read and study both analytically and synthetically — in one act, not two. What is at issue is *meditatio* whose secret is *oratio*. If free theologians begin with the Bible, this means that they begin with its witness and with the origin, theme, and content of this witness, which speaks to them through the witness, and which they let be spoken to them through it. Do they themselves speak in direct quotation from biblical verses and passages, or in exposition of them? Often perhaps, but perhaps not always. The freedom that the origin, theme, and content of the witness gives them can and must show itself in the need to try thinking and saying in their own words what they have heard in the Bible.

Theologische Studien 29, Zollikon–Zurich (1953), pp. 22f.

For the report of the Evanston World Council Meeting on "Christ the Hope of the World" (1954), Barth's seminar prepared a supplement on "The Hope of Israel."

We must first speak about the people who in its hope rests on the same subject as is the basis of our hope, the coming of the Messiah. This people is Israel. For three thousand years it has had a history that cannot be compared with that of any other people. After a brief ascendancy, it has trodden a path of suffering that is marked outwardly by war, defeat, captivity, suppression, dispersal, need, misery, and the most cruel persecution. Yet it will not and cannot perish until that hope is demonstrably fulfilled for it.

That hope is by nature different from hopes that rely on immanent processes or human programs. It is grounded in the promise God gave his chosen people. The content of this promise is that God will set up his kingdom on earth. It will dawn with the coming of the Messiah. The Messiah will appear in power and glory, gather the peoples, and execute judgment. With Israel as his chosen people, he will rule over the whole world. There will be eternal peace, and his kingdom will have no end.

The recent movement of Zionism and the establishment of the state of Israel in Palestine, although the origin is political, might well be seen as an expression that the hope is still very much alive today. That hope determines the content and nature of Judaism. If one can say of any society that it lives by hope, one must say it first of Judaism. Israel is the people of hope. Hope gives unity to its history. Without expectation of the Messiah who will come to set up his kingdom, there would no longer be any Judaism. God's faithfulness means that his promise is still valid (for Israel), and that this is still his chosen people. The fact that it has not perished proves it. For this twofold reason, if the church is to live according to its hope, it cannot bypass Judaism. Instead, Christians have often failed in this regard—approving, supporting, and even organizing Jewish persecutions. We confess that we have incurred great guilt thereby.

"Zur Erneuerung des Verhältnisses von Christen und Juden," *Handreichung* No. 39, Evangelische Kirche im Rheinland, pp. 104f.

Basel University celebrated its 500th anniversary in 1960. Because guests were not invited from behind the Iron Curtain, Barth refused to participate; but he wrote an article on "Systematische Theologie" for a Festschrift.

From the standpoint of its relation to the church, systematic theology is a church discipline, "church dogmatics." For the rest, it lives by the truth of the message of which it constantly has to remind itself and the church. It cannot try to prove the truth of God's Word either directly or indirectly. The triumph of this word inside and outside the church can never be its own work. It has to bear witness to its truth in a special way, by clinging to it. It has to trust that the truth will prove itself. This trust is its apologetic strength in relation to all Christian and non-Christian thought forms, myths, world views, and religions. In this trust it can meet them all, sure of its cause and therefore open, understanding, and patient, with good hope for those imprisoned in them. In this trust it tries to be true to its own law in the midst of other disciplines, to the utmost of its power doing basic and sober intellectual work. Grasped by this trust, systematic theology is

not only distinctively free, but for all the heavy responsibility and toil of its labors, it is free from worry, a cheerful science.
Lehre und Forschung an der Universität Basel, Basel (1960), p. 38.

Unable to write a requested article because of illness, Barth asked E. Busch to write an open letter addressed to the Christians of Southeast Asia, which he himself then signed (November 19, 1968).

Christians do good theology when they keep seriously to their theme. Good theologians are those who, cheerful and humble at one and the same time, acknowledge and confess with their diligent work and simple prayers: "I am the Lord thy God. Thou shalt have no other gods but me" (Ex. 20:3). Christian theology is good, then, when in all that is said, thought, and done, free from all Babylonian captivities, it is not an end in itself but service—service in which one learns constantly: "He must increase, but I must decrease" (Jn. 3:30). . . . When theologians serve him, they know that they must not cling to any standpoint, custom, or tradition, let alone look back like Lot's wife (Gen. 19:26), but always have cause to stride on ahead.

Christians do good theology when they keep to their theme cheerfully and with good humor. Let us have no cross theologians, nor boring theology! I know, of course, that there are today many very serious questions and that we all have big doubts. But since good theologians do not serve themselves but God, since they do not proclaim themselves but God, their questions and doubts must have no final power over them. Nor must they try to support their heavenly Father with any well-meaning apologetics, but with confidence and gladness they must believe that God is not really dead and will thus himself see to the acknowledgment of his name, his will, and his kingdom. I also know that there are many sad things all around us, and we ourselves are often not very cheerful companions. But since good theologians do not serve themselves but the Father of Jesus Christ, they may look with gladness and hope on those whom God at least loved, and even on themselves. And as they take their theme seriously, in spite of everything they may laugh heartily, and even laugh at themselves.

Offene Briefe 1945–1968, Zurich (1984), pp. 553f.

II. The Crisis of All Powers
"Dreadfully religious"

*B*ARTH WAS UNCOMFORTABLE *with religious forms. A friend who attended a service he conducted once gave him an A for preaching and a D for worship. Yet he took pains with his prayers and valued public worship highly. His understanding of prayer and worship explains his discomfort. Prayer for him was a yes to the living God, a confession both of relationship with God and of difference from him. Things are "dreadfully religious" when invocation of God is viewed as a private matter, when disposition is everything and obedience to God is evaded. All religion is open to this peril. Faith, and even God, can be bound up with alien goals and thus given distorted expression. Barth's discomfort with religion derived from a concern that the living God would not be invoked and life therefore frustrated. At Safenwil on October 9, 1917, Barth gave an address on "Religion and Life" to his own and Thurneysen's students. He published it in 1952 on the occasion of Günther Dehn's 70th birthday.*

As a matter of mood and sentiment, religion does not impinge on life, where what counts is power and force. Religion is alien to life. We have to bear the burden of this false situation in the church and the school. We preach opinions and create moods. We may succeed, but what do we really accomplish? Even if we speak powerfully and not as the scribes, even if power goes forth from us . . . it does not affect life, and no one takes it seriously, however deep an impression we make. It does not amount to anything serious. Only power is serious. Thus capitalism has never taken religion seriously. It has quietly built churches and schools without the slightest fear that it will raise up any dangerous counter-force by so doing. Militarism takes religion with so little seriousness that it quietly appoints chaplains who can pass on their sentiments between bombardments. . . . Socialism kindly says that religion is a private matter and patiently takes note of a few parsons who are Social Democrats without being afraid of the force that they might exert or that one day this force might seriously compete with its own power. No one takes religion seriously. The idea that it is something real, that it might have something to do with real power—no such idea exists in the world. . . . We ourselves see this. Above all, the Bible saw it, and the prodigal son (Lk. 15:11–32) laughs at us and declares war on us when we interpret him in terms of mood and sentiment. And then our situation becomes extremely critical.

Evangelische Theologie 11, Munich (1951–52), pp. 448f.

Barth published the first edition of his Romans *in 1919 and worked on a revised edition from autumn 1920 to summer 1921. In this second edition, opposing current trends, he tried to understand the gospel and the church on a biblical basis. (Barth never approved of the description of his further theological work as "dialectical theology.") The edition made him much sought after, and he found many associates, pupils, and critics.*

God is the unknown God. As such he gives to all life and breath and all things. His power is neither a natural nor a spiritual power, nor one of the higher or highest powers that we know or might know, nor the supreme power, nor their sum, nor fount. It is the crisis of all powers, the wholly other, compared to which they are something and nothing, nothing and something. It is their primary mover and their final rest. It is the origin that raises them all up and the goal that establishes them all. . . . The power of God, the institution of Jesus as Christ . . . is in the strict sense a *prepositing*, with no conceivable content. It takes place in the spirit and must be known in the spirit. It is self-sufficient, unconditioned, and intrinsically true. It is the absolutely new thing that is the decisive, transforming factor in human thinking about God. . . . All the teaching, morality, and cultus of the Christian community relate to this message insofar as they all seek to be only a shell crater or vacuum in which the message presents itself. The Christian community knows no intrinsically holy words, works, or things. It knows only words, works, and things that as negations point to the Holy One. What is Christian does not relate to the gospel but is a human by-product, a dangerous relic, a sorry misunderstanding, if it wants to be content instead of vacuum.

Der Römerbrief, Zurich (1984), pp. 11f. (ET London [1963], cf. p. 36).

Barth gave his first lectures on dogmatics as Honorary Professor of Reformed Theology at Goettingen in 1924. Forbidden by the faculty to use the title Dogmatik, *he imitated Calvin and called these lectures* Unterricht in der christlichen Religion.

You have probably never heard me use the words "religion" or "religiousness" except when quoting the thoughts of others, when it is apposite. . . . In what follows I do not propose to advance my own view of religion. I have no interest in this concept, not even enough to participate in efforts to give it new significance or content. This would not be impossible. In the rendering that philologists usually give the word *religio* today—i.e., awe, regard, respect, or reverence—I might with the help of a little dialectical accommodation claim it as a master concept for what I call faith and obedience, and in my view with more right than Schleiermacher had for what he understood by it. But for me the term is too freighted and stained with all the nonsense that has been made of it during the last two hundred years, and above all, I think, the apologetic nonsense. I can no longer hear or pronounce the word "religion" without the adverse recollection that in modern intellectual history it has in fact been a flag denoting the place of refuge to which Protestant and a good deal of Roman Catholic theology began a more or less headlong retreat when it no longer had the courage to think in terms of its object, that is, the Word of God, but was glad to find at the place where the little banner of religion waved a small field of historical and psychological reality to which, renouncing all else, it could devote itself as a true "as though" theology, at peace with the modern understanding of science. Behind the alien word "religion" and all that it entails, and also behind the word "piety," which some prefer, there lies concealed either shamefully or shamelessly the confession that as moderns we no longer dare to speak about God in principle, primarily, and with uplifted voice. Even with the best dialectical accommodation, I cannot today detach this historical background from even the better sense of the word *religio*. Perhaps a time will come when we can again speak about religion, as Calvin and Zwingli did, innocuously and uninhibitedly and without having to blush. But today is another day.

Unterricht in der christlichen Religion, Zurich (1985), pp. 223–225.

In December 1931, Barth wrote on "Fragen an das Christentum" in the Zofinger Zentralblatt.

The present situation, the conflict between new and old religions, finally and especially puts to Christianity the question of whether it understands itself. Is its proclamation real proclamation in contrast to that of the religions? Does it really believe, and believe aright, and say aright, what it has to say as it takes the offensive and responds to the religions with mission? If it has properly understood itself, then it cannot want to be Christendom or Christianity. Such terms make it one religion among others. Perhaps not even that, perhaps a world view inferior to the religions in power. Does Chris-

tianity realize that it is something different from what any
world view or religion can be? Does it see that it is the church
of the one God, the church of Jesus Christ, the church of the
God who has mercy on the lost? Amid all the loquacious
splendor of the religions, a Christianity that understands itself as the church will try to be the place where people *hear*
and *God* speaks. When revelation is present, everything depends on good hearing, rehearing, and better hearing. Mission to the religions must begin with the admission by Christianity that it knows what the preachers of the religions do
not know, namely, that in the service of the one true God we
are all poor, that we have not found God and never will, that
we can never do more than wait for God to find us. Knowing
this poverty, Christians know their solidarity with communists, fascists, and the adherents of all other religions.
They share the same need and realize that in it there is only
one hope. They share the same questions, to which the
religions, to the curse of humanity, can give only their sinister, demonic, and false answers. Those who believe in God's
revelation and know that they must listen and God must
speak, are automatically bound up, as it were, with all others.
In their alien religions they see the common need and questions that the others do not see. Bound up with them, they
can speak to them with authority. If the church listens to
God's Word, it is the church and not a society engaging in
propaganda. It has a mission; it is sent. It need not keep silent, for it may not. It may give offense, for it must. It need
not worry about itself. What it has to say to people on the
right hand and on the left, whether they like it or not, is gospel, not law. It will preach forgiveness and no obedience but
that which springs from forgiveness. It will not oppose a
Christian system to religious systems. It will not strive
against the religions as they strive on their own behalf.
Speaking with authority, it will proclaim freedom: freedom of
conscience and freedom for others, which the religions take
away and only the one true God can restore. It will proclaim
this freedom not as an ideal but as a Christmas gift: You *may*
be redeemed from bondage to demons because you *are* al-

ready redeemed. It will thus preach grace as grace. Does
Christianity do this? Is this its place and manner and message? Does it know that it is, and is it ready to be, the church
of Jesus Christ? This is the question that is put more urgently
than ever to Christianity today.

Theologische Fragen und Antworten, Zurich (1957), pp. 98f.

*On July 22, 1933, at Bonn, just before the church elections at which
Barth supported candidates opposed to the Hitler regime, he gave an
address entitled "For the Freedom of the Gospel."*

They [the German Christians] tell us as unequivocally as
possible that the proclamation of the gospel both draws and
must draw from two different sources. Holy Scripture is one,
and the other is the "historical hour," the present political situation, the experience of the German revolution of 1933.
With one eye the church must learn from this what God's
word is, just as it learns it with the other eye from the Bible.
As the Roman Catholic church has always said, there is the
book of nature and the book of grace. For the German Christians the book of nature is the event of January 30 and all that
it implies. . . . We cannot understand this enterprise as
reformation. It is deformation, not reformation. In it the
church does not have the single eye that is demanded. It is
squinting. Alongside God it sets a second god with an in-
dependent authority, namely, the Germans and their understanding of themselves and their concerns. But alongside
God there can be no other God, or God ceases to be God, and
all that we really have are two idols. The gospel preached by
the German Christians is in classical form an unfree gospel.
Faith is not decided by the call of God alone, nor is it our only
comfort in life and in death. Alongside God the giver, Germans are honored as the necessary and proper vessel for saving grace. But if the gospel is no longer free, it has ceased to
be gospel. Hence we have to say at this point a radical and

unconditional no: no to the starting point of this thinking, and no to all that follows therefrom.

Theologische Existenz heute 2, Munich (1933), pp. 11f.

In 1938, Barth published Kirchliche Dogmatik *I,2. He dealt with revelation and religion in § 17. Revelation, the objective basis of the divine–human relationship, he defined as the history of the covenant denoted by the name of Jesus Christ. This abolished religion as the basis of the relation but made a place for it if we refer it to the appropriate response to revelation that God makes possible.*

If man tries to grasp at truth of himself, he tries to grasp at it *a priori*. But in that case he does not do what he has to do when the truth comes to him. He does not believe. If he did, he would listen; but in religion he talks. If he did, he would accept a gift; but in religion he takes something for himself. If he did, he would let God himself intercede for God; but in religion he ventures to grasp at God. Because it is a grasping, religion is the contradiction of revelation, the concentrated expression of human unbelief, that is, an attitude and activity which is directly opposed to faith. It is a feeble but defiant, an arrogant but hopeless, attempt to create something which man could do, but now cannot do, or can do only because and if God himself creates it for him: the knowledge of the truth, the knowledge of God. We cannot, therefore, interpret the attempt as a harmonious cooperating of man with the revelation of God, as though religion were a kind of outstretched hand which is filled by God in his revelation. Again, we cannot say of the evident religious capacity of man that it is, so to speak, the general form of human knowledge, which acquires its true and proper content in the shape of revelation. On the contrary, we have here an exclusive contradiction. In religion man bolts and bars himself against revelation by providing a substitute, by taking away in advance the very thing which has to be given by God. . . .

He has, of course, the power to do this. But what he
achieves and acquires in virtue of this power is never the
knowledge of God as Lord and God. It is never the truth. It
is a complete fiction, which has not only little but no relation
to God. It is an anti-God who has first to be known as such
and discarded when the truth comes to him. But it can be
known as such, as a fiction, only as the truth does come to
him. . . .

Revelation does not link up with human religion which
is already present and practiced. It contradicts it, just as religion previously contradicted revelation. It displaces it, just as
religion previously displaced revelation; just as faith cannot
link up with a mistaken faith, but must contradict and dis-
place it as unbelief, as an act of contradiction.

Kirchliche Dogmatik I,2, Zurich (1983), pp. 330f. (ET Edinburgh [1956] pp.
302f.).

*On August 23, 1948, Barth addressed the World Council at Amster-
dam on the subject "The World's Disorder and God's Plan of Salvation." He reversed the title in his development of the theme.*

God's plan of salvation is above—the world's disorder,
our explanations of it, our proposals and plans to combat it,
all these are below. If we are really to know its nature (and
that of the church with it), we can see and grasp it only from
above, only in the light of God's saving plan. On the other
hand, from the disorder of the world and our Christian analy-
ses and postulates regarding it, there is no glimpse of God's
plan nor way to it. . . . We are right to warn our brethren,
the people of our time, against the danger that technological
problems and solutions will cause them to forget that they
themselves are part of the evil that they are trying to overcome along these lines . . . to forget that they are the accused and not the judge, to forget that human existence
makes no sense apart from a transcendent truth, righteous-

ness, and love that they themselves do not create but by which they can only let themselves be bound. But in these three matters, how about the beam in our own eye (Mt. 7:3), and how can we help these brethren of ours if we stiffly adopt a positivistic mode of thought that has nothing whatever to do with the Christian realism demanded of us? . . . Do we not have to realize that God's plan of salvation is really *his* plan, that is, his kingdom that has already come and is victorious and has been set up in all its majesty: our Lord Jesus Christ, who has robbed sin, the devil, and hell of their power, and vindicated divine and human right in his own person? That we are not to understand by God's plan the church's existence in the world, its task in the face of the world's disorder, its outer and inner activity as the instrument of a better human life, or finally the success of its work in Christianizing the human race and setting up an order of peace and justice that will embrace our whole planet? That God's plan of salvation is not to be regarded as a kind of Christian Marshall plan? If it were, then obviously the lordship of Jesus Christ at the Father's right hand, as well as the rule of God's providence, would have come under the rule and control of Christianity, and troubled humanity would be awaiting salvation from our historical acuity, from the programs and activities and the future triumph of the church as the embodiment and representative of Jesus Christ and therefore of God himself. We would then easily begin to think that we must act as though the good Lord were dead, as though there were at least no divine wisdom, righteousness, goodness, will, or plan above our own entity as Christianity and the church, as though these things were present only in the form of our own views, insights, and purposes, of our Christian efforts to do justice to God and our neighbors. No wonder we would then have to be so nervous and affrighted when we saw the world's disorder, just as Peter was when he saw the waves and the storm into which he began to sink at once (Mt. 14:30). . . . Here is the final root and basis of all human dis-

order: the dreadful, godless, ridiculous idea that humanity is
the Atlas that is ordained to hold up the vault of heaven.
Theologische Existenz heute, NS 15, Munich (1949), pp. 3–5.

*At the end of August 1958, Barth wrote to a pastor in East Germany
about the situation of pastors in that country.*

Not some abstract idea, theory, deity, or its law, but the
free grace of God which is mighty from eternity and has ap-
peared in Jesus Christ is what you must fear and love above
all things. God and his free grace are really above all the
thoughts and ideas and habits with which we Christians
everywhere have lived thus far concerning what seemed to
serve his glory and human salvation. We have unavoidably
taken so many things for granted. The existence of a church
guaranteed or respected or at least tolerated by society and
the state, with its own established place in the social fabric.
Sunday as a day of rest and worship, and Christian fes-
tivals. . . . Infant baptism, confirmation, marriage, and bur-
ial as Christian signposts in every life. . . . The church's influence on public education . . . either with the maximum
claim that schools must be Christian or the minimal claim that
there be no opposition to Christianity. . . . The prestige and
dignity of the church's representatives. . . . Their formal
freedom to speak, whether directly or indirectly, whether
sought or unsought, on human affairs in general. If Christianity has never been wholly uncontested (not even in the
last centuries), it has seemed the most natural thing in the
world to us that the proclamation of the gospel of Jesus Christ
should take place in these channels and that everything possible should be done to uphold and defend them (for the sake
of God and the gospel!). And this has been done amply and
zealously enough, with more or less skill and success. Behind
this whole attempt, is there not the assumption that nor-
mally, at least under the title of the free exercise of religion,

the Christian cause and confession should be formally recognized and respected by each and all? That the world as such is obliged to grant Christianity the right to exist within it?
Offene Briefe 1945–1968, Zurich (1984), pp. 423f.

On April 27, 1963, Barth addressed some 300 foreign students in Basel on the theme "Christianity and Religion."

I have to come before you as a theologian, that is, as the representative of a discipline that most of you will hardly know of even by name or rumor. Universities in many countries do not pursue it. Even in Basel and the rest of Switzerland and Europe it has a fairly modest role. We have to realize, of course, that it was once the controlling center of all academic research and teaching in the West. But that rested on a misunderstanding that we do not wish to recur. If there is any discipline that both inwardly and outwardly ought to serve, it is theology. It lives by the hidden radiance of the object it addresses, not by any fame that it acquires in dealing with this object. . . .

Here in Basel, as in the rest of Europe, you will find many expressions of what we usually call Christianity: church buildings, institutions, courts, societies, organizations, publications, and people who profess that they are Christians. The Christianity that is more or less visible in all this is the specific affair of theology. But if you think it worthwhile to find the proper way of looking at this and understanding it, be careful. You will probably at once associate the word "Christianity" with the general concept of religion. The matter will probably look like one of those bold but ambiguous and sinister attempts of people to gain an emotional, conceptual, or practical master concept of deity, of deity as that which transcends our own nature and history, and indeed the whole physical and spiritual cosmos. Karl Marx was not wrong when he regarded religion as one of the undertakings that tries to provide a desirable ideological superstructure for hu-

man life and society, something that will undergird and uphold them. But we radically misunderstand Christianity if we
regard or explain it as one such superstructure and therefore
as a religion. Christianity is no religion. Everything human
about it, all the expressions in which it might seem to resem-
ble a religion, are simply the echo or reflection of the movement of a very different subject that does not originate with
us or lead from us, but which comes to us and to which we
have to respond. Alone among the religions Christianity is
essentially a backward, forward, and upward pointer to the
movement of this different subject, which differs from all religion and is the direct opposite of every human superstructure, of every religion.

If we understand Christianity—which is, incidentally, the
task of theology—in its true essence, that is, in terms of its
historical sources, the records of its origin in the Old and
New Testaments, we cannot close our eyes to the fact that
what we have here, in antithesis to all religions, is not a human movement to God but a divine movement to humanity.
In these records we do not find people who are striv-
ing . . . to do justice to a supreme being in the form of
crude or refined ideas of God and various cultic and moral
ways of serving him. Instead, we find people who are
claimed by the fact that, on their behalf and that of the whole
world, the so-called transcendent has become immanent before their very eyes and ears. The one, true, living God—he
is that very different subject—rose up in all his power before
people ever thought of him or sought him or caused him to
do so. He, the free God, acted, acts, and will act; spoke,
speaks, and will speak—and all to take humanity to himself,
to take up its cause and bring it to fulfillment. He the free
God, but gracious in his freedom; he who exists in this world
in the earthly history of him from whom Christianity takes its
name; he who in the man Jesus Christ gives the one proof of
his existence beside which there can be no other. Christianity
is originally and essentially present to this day wherever people are summoned by this God and powerfully awakened by
him to faith and love and hope, thus becoming obedient to

him. True Christianity consists, or rather, takes place where active attention is paid to the work and word of God. It thus begins where all religion ends, where religion is fundamentally overcome. The worst fall of theology occurred, incidentally, when it began to understand and present itself as the science of religion. . . .

And now here in Europe you will come up against the signs of what we call Christianity. May they be authentic signs of authentic Christianity! May you not confuse them with signs of our religion! Apart from the fact that we want to be Christians and to call ourselves such, we are all religious too, and at times even dreadfully religious. There are religions disguised as science, art, politics, technology, sport, and fashion . . . also mammon, money, the most powerful of these concealed but very real deities. Let no one lead you to think that here you are in the sphere of a Christian tradition, civilization, or culture, the "Christian West"! Essentially, to be Christian is to be governed by the gospel of Jesus Christ, by the liberating knowledge of God's gracious coming to the human race. This knowledge is an event, not a state, not an institution, not a predicate with which one might adorn and characterize human constructs. Even here we are not really governed by this event but at best only touched by it from afar. We still have to learn in truth what is meant by genuine Christianity, by the event of glad conversion in which God precedes and we follow, God the Lord and we his servants, God the Father and we his children. We still have to learn what is meant by Jesus Christ. There is a religious West but not a Christian West. There are only Western people confronted by Jesus Christ.

But they are confronted by Jesus Christ, whether or not they know where they come from, what open or concealed religion they belong to, what manner or disposition they are of. Jesus Christ died for all and lives for all. The work of God done in him and the word of God spoken in him are for all. Essential Christianity is the horizon and hope of all of us. It might be that one day this will be better understood and lived out in Asia and Africa than in Europe. For the moment try to learn, not from us but with us, that God for us and God with us are the horizon and hope of all of us. Try to learn what genuine Christianity is as the glad conversion and establishment of all religion. The little bit of theology that I have now presented to you ought at least to stir you to think about this.

Kirchenblatt für die reformierte Schweiz 119. Jahrgang, Basel (1963), pp. 181–183.

III. Faith by the Decision of Jesus Christ

"Either—Or"

*T*HOSE WHO PRESENT US WITH an "either–or" demand that we decide. *Such a summons puts us in an existential situation: "Thou art the man" (2 Sam. 12:7). Barth learned this from Kierkegaard. But as he grew older he focused on the decision made once for all by Jesus Christ at the cross (Rom. 6:10). God has already decided for us in Christ, and all he now asks is that we should obediently acknowledge, recognize, and confess this divine decision. When believers apply this in their lives, Jesus Christ is for them the reality of both church and world. At Safenwil (1911–1921) Barth had seen increasingly that radical renewal is needed before God. He thus had had to speak about God more radically and decisively. He did this in a sermon on Ezekiel 13:1–16 (February 6, 1916), which he printed privately and distributed to every house in the parish. By 1932, however, he confessed that this sermon was more legal than evangelical, not setting the human situation under God's Word, but using God's Word. He thus advised young pastors who might understandably like the sermon not to follow his example* (Reformierte Kirchenzeitung 18. Jahrgang [1967] p. 204).

You expect your pastor to be easygoing, someone you can live with as you are, whose sermons will finally amount to no more than what sound common sense thinks and says, for example, in the newspaper. You respect the Bible, but you think that when it is opened you will simply find beautiful stories and sayings, for example, about Canaan or David or the Savior. You can listen to it comfortably and with enjoyment, and peacefully slumber within, because it was all said and it all took place many years ago and many miles away, and basically does not concern you. . . .

If I were to give a name to what you want, I would say that you want a false prophet, for this is exactly how false prophets are described in the Bible.

And now you are disturbed because you see more and more clearly that things are not as you think. You begin to note that Christianity refuses to adorn our present life, that it confronts our life, and puts to us the question: Either–Or? You or I? You begin to see that the church is not one house among others. You cannot go in and come out peacefully. What takes place there, what comes to light there, critically disturbs the balance of your life and acts and fatally jolts your quiet conscience. . . . You begin to note that you have a *pastor* in the village, that is, a man who most uncomfortably questions everything and has to give unexpected answers to all questions, a man about whom you are never really sure, like a meteor of unknown whence and whither. You begin to see that it is a great and dangerous thing when the Bible is really opened . . . and when, like a river that bursts its banks, it spreads destruction and yet also fertility everywhere, overthrowing old things and everywhere creating new things, as it has done since the days of Abraham. . . .

Look, you begin to see all these things, and it unsettles you. You compare it with your own picture of a pastor, church, Bible, and religion, and you want me to be different, to correspond to that picture. . . .

Let me tell you first that I understand your disquiet very well. I am really distressed myself that I must think and speak this way. From month to month it has been a new and unheard of thing for me that God alone wills thus to be right and righteous. I would often have liked to evade this insight, for it is too high and difficult for me. Everything in my position and words that you now think is directed against you was really directed against me and my own life long before. What bothers you about me bothers me first, namely, that God's Word cannot accept our life and world and thoughts and habits and acts and omissions and justice and injustice just as they are. . . .

This is why you must make a decision, a choice.

One possibility is that you may resolutely set God's will aside. This makes some sense. Why not honestly admit it? I do not want what God wants. I want this life, not the new life. Why shouldn't many of you now resolve, perhaps from this day on, never to go to church again, to get rid of the pastor, to turn the church into a gymnasium or factory, since what takes place there is fundamentally very unacceptable and repugnant . . . ?

The other possibility is to let yourselves be overcome and taken captive by God's will. You can enter with me into the great unrest that is unavoidable when God speaks to us. This too makes sense. You can help me bear the burden of God alone counting and God alone being right. You can help me call upon him, strive for him, joy in him, and sigh for him. You will then be helping not me but God and yourselves. Today I again invite you to tread this path with me. Be reconciled to God. Walk in the light while you have it, and thus be children of the light. This too will be sensible and understandable. You will show by it that you have grasped the Either–Or.

You cannot take a middle course, the golden mean. Not your pastor but God himself prevents you with all his might. You cannot demand that I should tell you about God and also accept things as they are. This is impossible. You must choose one of the two: one, not both. Decide! And if I have put it clearly enough, and you have heard me, decide today!

"Der Pfarrer . . . ," Zofingen (1916), pp. 7–8, 15f.

Barth was always attracted to the portrayal of John the Baptist on Grünewald's Isenheim altarpiece. He found in the elongated index finger, denoting Christ as the Lamb of God, a graphic symbol of the function of the witness, who must decrease as Christ increases (Jn.

3:30). For some fifty years he kept a copy of this depiction over his desk as a "visual aid." His address "The Word of God and the Word of Man in Christian Preaching" at Königsberg (November 25, 1924) and Danzig (November 26, 1924) deals with the church's task of bearing witness to God's revelation.

What God has said to me, I cannot group with other things that are said by others, not even at the head of the group. Otherwise it is not *said*, to *me*, by *God*. What God has said to me *eo ipso* rivets me and claims me and takes me captive, ruling out all discussion or contradiction or even comparison or objective consideration. All the reasons with which we might try to explain why God's Word deserves precedence compared with other words can only come later. God's Word establishes its own validity by being spoken to me. It excludes every why or wherefore. Otherwise, it is not God's Word. I can resist, negate, or refuse obedience, but I cannot question the fact that the concept "God's Word" has this categorical quality. The word that is spoken to us in baptism, God's address that the Christian church believes it hears, is constituted thus. It is . . . a specific word, as unique and specific as our own existence. . . . In response to it, only offense or faith is possible, only obedience or revolt. A word that admits of any other response is not God's Word. The church is the community that is addressed and challenged by this specific word. In this sense it calls the Bible God's Word. . . .

The church stands in the tradition of John the Baptist. What it can and should do is point an outstretched finger: "Behold the Lamb of God, that taketh away the sin of the world."

Zwischen den Zeiten 3. Jahrgang, Munich (1925), pp. 123, 130.

On May 23, 1937, Barth preached at St. James, Basel, on John 2:23–3:21.

The point in each case is that Jesus speaks and the others are silent. Nicodemus begins a fine address to Jesus, even a Christian one about Jesus, but Jesus interrupts him . . . : "Truly, truly, I say to you. . . . " Nicodemus then asks questions, the kinds of questions we know so well, and Jesus does not pursue them but ignores them: "Truly, truly, I say to you. . . . " Herein already is his whole benefit for us. He treats us as though we had not spoken, and speaks himself. Perhaps this is the best thing that is said in the story of Nicodemus. Perhaps this is what saved him. Perhaps this was his faith, about which we are not told, but which God saw, namely, that he kept silence and let Jesus speak. When the point comes when we must be silent, when we must rein in our speaking, even our fine speaking, even our Christian speaking, even our ever so important and serious questions, when we must listen, when we must let Jesus speak—then we are together with Jesus and in the process of conversion. . . .

What does conversion mean? What can it mean but faith? And what can faith mean but receiving the gift of comfort that the Comforter has promised and offered us? What can faith mean but accepting and endorsing God's chosen way of love, not wanting to be anything other than the world that is so loved by him, and therefore letting Jesus and Jesus alone be our conversion? Not wanting to be the heroes of our own conversion stories, not even half so, not even to the smallest degree? All that we have to do is believe in Jesus.

Fürchte dich nicht! Predigten aus den Jahren 1934 bis 1948, Munich (1949), pp. 129f., 133f.

In March 1937, Barth gave ten lectures on "The Knowledge of God" at Aberdeen University in Scotland, and in 1938 he gave another ten on "The Service of God." He based his lectures on the Scots Confession of 1560.

Precisely as our future, Jesus Christ necessarily determines our present as well. Today to expect him as judge means to believe in him and hence to let him be our righteousness and our life. The comfort of believers, the comfort of the warring and suffering church in the present, is that since we do not have to fear Jesus Christ, we do not have to fear anyone or anything; for he is Lord of all, of the whole world. . . . Faith has nothing to fear except that it might cease to be faith and change into unbelief, error, or superstition. One may know all false belief by the fact that it holds out other hopes apart from and alongside Jesus Christ, and that those who have it cling to such other hopes. In so doing, no matter how great or beautiful these hopes may be, they fall away from fellowship with their Savior and back into sin and under its curse. They will now have to fear Jesus Christ, and so they will now have to be afraid in the world and among others as well. The present of all false faith is a joyless present; this fact may be hidden, but it is nonetheless real, for the future of this present is darkness. Faith has no power to uphold and sustain itself as faith. Such a faith would be a false faith trying to live in its own strength. True faith lives in the power of Jesus Christ himself. Hence true faith does not need to fear that it might become false faith. . . .

Who, then, has faith? How can anyone have faith? How does anyone come to faith . . . ?

If faith is the life of those who meet Jesus Christ as him from whom alone they receive salvation, then one can understand . . . that those who live in faith, encountering the faithfulness of God, find themselves convicted of their own unfaithfulness. They see that they are in no position to believe in themselves or to ascribe to themselves a capacity or power by means of which they might achieve their own salvation or cooperate in achieving it. . . . That people are more or less religiously inclined, if true, might well be a good thing. But those who really have faith will never regard their faith as an actualization or expression of their religious life. Instead they will confess that their religious capacity as such would have led them to gods and idols but in no way to Jesus Christ. Those who really have faith know only that it is impossible for them to believe on their own. It is only unbelievers who imagine that faith is a human possibility, concerning which they might then say that it happens to have been denied them personally. And even supposed believers who see in their faith the actualization of a human possibility are in truth unbelievers of that kind. Faith is not an art. Faith is not an achievement. Faith is not a good work of which some may boast while others can excuse themselves with a shrug of the shoulders for not being capable of it. It is a decisive insight of faith itself that all of us are incapable of faith in ourselves, whether we think of its preparation, beginning, continuation, or completion. In this respect believers understand unbelievers, skeptics, and atheists better than they understand themselves. Unlike unbelievers they regard the impossibility of faith as necessary, not accidental. . . .

True service of God consists of believing in Jesus Christ, accepting the fact that he lives his life in our place and for us. But his life as the life of the Head is not to be separated from the life of the body, the life of the One from the life of the many. If his life is ours, then our life has to be the life of members of his body. We cannot be outside. Because he is inside, we too are inside with him. We must be on guard against false analogies in this regard. One can be a good citizen without belonging to a political party. One can be a good musician without joining a choral society. One can be a philosopher and as an eclectic or skeptic hold aloof from all philosophical movements. But one cannot believe as a Christian without believing both within the church and with the church. The church is no party, society, or movement. The church is the form of existence of Christian faith, because this faith is faith in the One who died and rose again for the many. This content _must_ have and can _only_ have this form.

Gotteserkenntnis und Gottesdienst, Zollikon (1938), pp. 118f., 122f., 157f. (ET London [1938], cf. pp. 100, 105f., 154f.).

In March 1939, Barth spoke in several Dutch cities on "The Sovereignty of the Word of God and the Decision of Faith." Asked to avoid political references, he refused on the ground that theology is both implicitly and explicitly political. He was also unwilling to help in any way to promote a National Socialist Europe.

The decision of faith takes place in response to God's Word, on account of its sovereignty and in subjection to this sovereignty. Let us see to it that wittingly or unwittingly we do not substitute something else, that the decision and our obedience are not something other than faithful exposition and application of God's Word. How else could it be the decision of faith? How else could it be obedience? The important thing here is that the sovereignty of God's Word is marked by its exclusiveness. We are not yet obedient, or no longer so, if we are engaged in expounding the voice of our own heart or conscience or understanding. We are also not yet obedient, or no longer so, if the court to which we are finally responsible is a system, a program, a statute, a method, an "ism," no matter whether it be philosophical, political, or theological, static or dynamic, conservative, liberal, or authoritarian, or even Christian. Even at best an "ism" . . . is not God's Word, nor can it replace this. It cannot relieve us of the task of our own new responsibility to God's Word itself. . . . It can demand respect and grant instruction and direction. But it is subject to the judgment, verdict, and decision of God's own Word. We have to ask whether it serves the exposition of this Word, and we have to do so the more honestly the dearer it is to us. If it is not satisfied with at best a relative authority, this is a sign that the devil has invented it, or that it has become an instrument in the devil's hands. . . .

The decision of faith cannot, of course, anticipate the judgment, verdict and decision of the Word of God himself. God is in heaven, we on earth. The decision of faith takes place on earth and therefore in fear of the divine judgment and in need of the forgiveness of our past and future sins. It always means that we must responsibly venture to give the command of God's word a definite exposition and application. Only in great humility and in great joy can we do this. But we must do it. We must obey. We can obey only in the form of this decision and therefore only in the exposition and application of the command undertaken in fear, humility, and joy. In the process we shall always have the impression that it is far beyond our own insight or power to take the decision of faith. And we shall often have to accept the fact that by doing it we give others the impression of arrogance. But we are not asked about the wealth of our own resources; we are asked about our obedience and therefore about what we make of the pound entrusted to us. It is better to give the impression of arrogance than to stay neutral with an appearance of humility. Neutrality is really a decision of unbelief. How can the decision of faith be made without self-criticism or without openness to the criticism of others? But it must always be made, and for all the self-criticism and the criticism of perhaps the whole world, it may and must be made with a certainty that looks with uplifted head to the Judge who is also our Savior. How else can we be obedient as fallible and faulty beings?

Theologische Studien 5, Zollikon–Zurich (1939), 16f.,18.

After the war, Barth gave some guest lectures at Bonn in the summer of 1947. He also spoke to large audiences in cities such as Berlin and Dresden. In the address "Christus und wir Christen," he tried to indicate the necessary basis of German reconstruction.

Luther once said that we have not become Christians but are in process of becoming. Let me put this thought as follows: We are Christians when it takes place that Christ calls us to be Christians. We are not Christians merely as citizens of the so-called Christian West. We are not Christians as members of a so-called Christian nation. We are not Christians merely because we have grown up in a so-called Christian family and environment. Nor are we Christians because we have a so-called religious inclination. . . . We are also not Christians because we have a so-called Christian view of things, devote ourselves to a Christian moral code, or possibly have in mind a Christian program for church and state. One cannot be a Christian as one is a member of a party or society, nor is one a Christian merely as a member of the Roman Catholic, Lutheran, or Reformed church. These are things one has become, and they have nothing whatever to do with the call of Christ. . . .

We should begin by perceiving and experiencing God's mercy. It is a beginning that, among all those who do not yet believe or no longer believe, we have this faith. . . . Faith is a beginning in us too, for our perception and recognition of the divine promise and address always have the same relationship to these that the number one has to infinity. . . . Thus those who believe readily agree with what the man in the Gospel said: "Lord, I believe, help thou mine unbelief" (Mk. 9:24).

We Christians, then, differ from others. We do so because, as lost sinners among other lost sinners, we make this beginning, knowing better than they do that we are not better than they are. We may precede others in knowing better than they do that they and we can live *only* by God's mercy.

Theologische Existenz heute NF 11, Munich (1948), pp. 5,8.

In the winter of 1956–57, Barth lectured on Church Dogmatics *IV,3, which was published in two half volumes in 1959. In the second half especially he dealt with the witness of Christians and the Christian community.*

Faith in a synthesis always has as its basis the desire to find escape from decisions in the supposed freedom of the Yes and No, of the As-well-as, of the neutrality which is fa-

tally active in the origin of the combination of the good creation of God with nothingness and then again in the combination of this confusion with the world government of God. As
the community sees and knows, the decision has been made
in Jesus Christ which makes quite impossible the idle contem-
plation and assessment of world-occurrence from a specta-
tor's seat high above the antithesis between God and sinful
man. All mere meditation or discussion for discussion's sake
is now ruled out. . . . The community of Jesus Christ sees
the decision taken in him. It keeps to it. It follows it. It follows
it within world-occurrence and therefore within the limits of
its own possibilities. Yet it does follow it, not as an idle spec-
tator but in active obedience. It follows, not in one great absolute step, but in several small and relative steps. But it really
does follow it. It cannot and will not accomplish the coming
of the new man and his world and the perishing of the old
man and his. It can only attest this coming. But it does this
in resolute decisions for and against. It cannot and should not
be otherwise than that where it does there should be provi-
sional clarifications anticipating the great and conclusive clarity toward which it and the whole cosmos are mov-
ing. . . . Where two apparently equal and illuminating
possibilities seem to offer, it will . . . decide for the one and
not the other, and therefore against the other. Conversely, it
may . . . pursue or seek a third way. But in any case,
whether by declaration or impressive silence, whether by
partisanship or rejection of partisanship or even the formation of its own party, it will resolutely participate. And in so
doing it will always have regard to the decision taken in Jesus
Christ; it will always look back to the triumph of the cause of
God and man championed by him; it will always seek to respect and assert his great Yes and No as it freely speaks its
own little Yes and No; it will always look forward to the future, perfect manifestation of his victory, of the Yes and No
spoken in him. Looking backwards and forwards in this way,
it will exclude any compromises in the little Yes and No
which it can speak. . . . What it has been given to know in
a certain situation on the basis of the new reality of history in

Jesus Christ, it can never wrap up nor conceal nor keep to itself nor treat as if it were something indifferent, a mere matter of faith which can remain purely inward and individual and need not be followed by any specific conclusion or action. On the contrary, in concrete obedience and confession it will always do in world-occurrence that which men who do not yet know Jesus Christ neither do nor can do. It will take concrete account of the atonement made in Jesus Christ, the covenant fulfilled in him, the order re-established in him. It is always expected to do or refrain from doing specific things. And as it executes its decisions in world-occurrence, it will undoubtedly change it. "Resolves genuinely taken change the world" (C.F.v. Weizsäcker). They do not do so absolutely conclusively or unequivocally. What the community can say and do . . . will always be relative . . . the erection of a sign. But the point at issue is that there should be this relative alteration of world history by the erection of signs. The community cannot and must not evade this if its faith is not an indolent or dead faith, if it is faithful with the little possibilities entrusted to it in relation to the new reality of history. No more than this is demanded.

Kirchliche Dogmatik IV,3, Zurich (1979), pp. 822ff. (ET Edinburgh [1962], pp. 718ff.).

On Christmas Eve 1963, Barth preached on John 16:33 in Basel prison, where from 1954 on he felt more at home than in big churches. The sermon was broadcast live in Switzerland and southwest Germany.

I have overcome the world. This is the Christmas message. *I*—the child in the crib at Bethlehem tells us this—in great humility but also with great power and emphasis, *I*, the Son of God the Almighty Father, Creator of heaven and earth. *I*, who have given myself to you as the Son of Man, as one like yourselves, in order that God might be your God and

you his people, in order that the salvation, peace, and joy of
this covenant might be yours. *I* have overcome the world.
Not good or wicked people, not clever or stupid people, not
believers or unbelievers, not popes or councils or govern-
ments or universities, not science or technology. . . . *I*
have done it.

I have overcome the *world*. The Christmas message is for
the world. The world—this is our great house which was so
well and gloriously built and arranged as God's creation, but
which is now so full of darkness, a place of wickedness and
sorrow. The world—we are the world, whom God made so
good and destined to be his children, but who fell from him,
who became his enemies and enemies of each other and our
own enemies. This world God loved so much and in such a
way that he was willing to give me, his Son—says the child
of Bethlehem—and he actually did so (cf. Jn. 3:16).

I have *overcome* the world, this child says. It needed a
great Lord to do that. But he is this. A strange Lord, to be
sure, very different from the great lords who have thought
they could conquer and subject at least this or that part of the
world, reducing it by cunning or by force. A Lord who was
born a poor child away from home in a stall, and put in a crib
beside the ox and the ass—and who knows but what the
wood of this crib did not come from the same forest from
which the wood was later hewn to make his cross? For this
child overcame the world by giving up himself to a death of
shame on account of the world's sin and guilt. This is how he
rescued it from destruction. This is how he reconciled it to
God. This is how he won it for God. This is how he restored
it. This is how he made us more glorious than before.

I *have* overcome the world, we read. Not some day I will.
"It is finished" (Jn. 19:30), it has happened, it is done. The
only thing for you to do is to note the fact, and adjust to it
and build on it, that you live in a world that has been overcome, that you yourselves are people whom I have
overcome.

But wait. If Jesus Christ had not said this, it would all be
too good to be true. And he also tells us, and tells us first, as

we heard, that in the world we shall have anxiety and affliction. Anxiety and affliction are related to pressure. They
mean being pressed, hemmed in, under the threat of danger.
Our Lord does not tell us that we *may* or *should* or *must* have
anxiety and affliction. He does not reproach us for having
them. He simply affirms very soberly that in the world we
shall have anxiety and affliction.

Would we, perhaps, rather not hear this? Do we perhaps
think it does not fit in with the Christmas season, the carols,
the lights, the gifts? Look you, dear brothers, Christmas
would be totally dishonest, a great illusion, if we were not
ready to be told that in the world we shall have anxiety and
affliction. The child in the Bethlehem crib, who was smitten
on Golgotha's cross, tells us two things: first, that he has
overcome the world, and second, that in it we shall have
anxiety and affliction. If we shut our ears to the latter, we cannot hear and understand the former. Very honestly, then, we
must let what is said be said to us: In the world you shall have
anxiety and affliction, even the strong among you, even on
this holy eve.

Younger people are often anxious about themselves and
the life that lies ahead of them. . . . Older people are anxious about increasing physical and mental weaknesses.
. . . People of all ages are anxious in the presence of others
who are always wanting something or who encroach on them
too much; they are anxious in the press of crowds, in which,
oddly enough, they often feel lonely and lost. People are understandably anxious about heavy responsibilities in which
they might be set. . . . I need not hide the fact that . . . always . . . I am anxious when I have to preach. . . . There
is anxiety—and this is a serious matter—in face of the steady
passage of time, of the days, weeks, and years of these brief
lives of ours (Ps. 90:9f.). . . .

In short, we do have anxiety and affliction in the world.
It hardly needs a saying of the Lord to make us admit this and
accept its validity. It is so, and all the things we have indi-
cated just now add up to the fact that we are anxious about
life, or, we might say, about death; for our great anxiety is be-

fore the threat which we see presented to life on every hand
by death, by the total end that is intimated everywhere, by
our hopeless delivering up to nothingness. We are anxious in
the face of the night when no one can work (cf. Jn. 9:4). There
are, to be sure, many petty, unnecessary, passing anxieties;
but strictly these are all signs or symptoms of the great anxiety about life and death that we all have, deeply hidden perhaps, yet still all of us.

Dear brothers, this Christmas Eve, to prepare to receive
the Christmas message, we must relentlessly accept and admit the fact that in the world we shall have anxiety. But
enough of that. The very one who says it, the child in the crib
and the man on the cross, calls unmistakably across the troubled sea of our anxiety: "But be of good cheer."

Here again we have a powerful and lordly "but" as we do
so often in the Bible. It brings to our attention something un-
deniably and unshakably true. When we are told that "with
men this is impossible" (Mt. 19:26), or that "the mountains
may depart and the hills be removed" (Is. 54:10), or that
"heaven and earth will pass away" (Mt. 24:35), or that "the
Lord has chastened me" (Ps. 118:18), a second statement im-
mediately follows; it does not negate or strike out or erase the
first but reduces and overshadows it: "But with God all
things are possible" (Mt. 19:26); "but my grace shall not depart from you" (Is. 54:10); "but my words will not pass away"
(Mt. 24:35); "but he has not given me over to death" (Ps.
118:18). So also here: "But be of good cheer."

Be of good cheer. This does not mean, think of something
else; ignore what causes you anxiety by distracting yourself
with business or some wild enterprise. You neither can nor
will escape it, no more than you can escape yourself. And
note that the useless and impossible attempt to flee from
anxiety is usually the cause of all kinds of evil and new
suffering.

Be of good cheer. This means: Lift up your eyes to the
hills from which help comes to you (Ps. 121:1). Look ahead
to the next few steps on your way and then step out and take
courage, and even be a little cheerful, just where you are in

the middle of anxiety, even that great anxiety in the face of
life and death that you all undoubtedly know. Can we do
this? Is this more than the counsel and promise of a well-
meaning person—advice that we do not need and can make
nothing of in practice? Certainly, none of us can be of good
cheer, or even try to be, by means of our own invention, insight, or resolve. But all of us can if we will listen to him who
as the true Son of God and Man came into the world in which
we have anxiety and suffered the supreme anxiety in it: "My
God, my God, why hast thou forsaken me?" (Mk. 15:34), but
who overcame this world, reconciled it to God, and thus set
a limit to the anxiety that we all have. Because of this limit,
there shines for us, his people walking in darkness, a great
light (Is. 9:1). As we see this light and follow it . . . at his
word we are free to be of good cheer, free for a great calm,
not before or after, but *in* the storm of our anxiety, when we
are in great distress and see no way out.

To the question whether we can be of good cheer, as the
Lord says, a second answer may be given. Since none of us
can be of good cheer of ourselves, none of us can be so alone.
Without exception, all those who gather with his people are
told, not privately but as its members, that they may and
should be of good cheer. . . . Can you really, even in anxiety and affliction, hear the angels sing and say: "Glory to God
in the highest"? The test is: Can you also hear them sing and
say: "Peace on earth" (Lk. 2:14)? Peace in this house. Peace
between you and the one behind you. Peace between the
man in this cell and the man in that. Peace between the
prisoners and the wardens. Peace between those here and
their relatives at home. Can you really look up and ahead?
You may if you do not fail to look also right and left to your
neighbors, who would also like to look up and ahead and
perhaps need your help. Can you really cling to Jesus Christ
as your Savior and believe in him? You will if you do not see
in those around you, likable or not, a mere mass of people but
the community that Jesus Christ, the common Savior, loved
and called. Can you be sure that you are a child of God (cf.
1 Jn. 3:1) in the midst of the world and its anxiety? You may

and should with full certainty if you treat others as your brothers because they are brothers of Jesus Christ and therefore children of God. Here are tests for all of us. But why should we not all meet these tests?

Prayer. Lord Jesus Christ, if all is not to be in vain, thou must thyself come to us now and speak to us about the glory of what for us thou wert and didst, what thou art and dost, what thou wilt be and wilt do—and also about the sober truth that in the world we shall have anxiety and affliction, but above all about the glad hope in which we may cling to thee now and forever. We are so deaf and dumb. Open our ears that we may hear and our lips that we may be witnesses for thee to each other.

Speak thy word to us all so that we may be gathered together and become thy people, thy community. Speak it to each of us that we may not merely be called Christians but continually become Christians. Speak it to all our relatives at home, to all prisoners in all earth's prisons, to the sick, the suffering, and the dying in hospitals, to the many who are agitated, provoked, or exhausted this Christmas season, to the sad, the defiant, the over-superficial, the over-thoughtful, the over-credulous, and the over-cynical, to parents and children, teachers, authors, and journalists, members of our councils and courts, to pastors and their congregations, to the great and strong and also to the little and weak in every nation. We all have need that thou speak it to us as thou alone canst speak it. And so grant us all a good Christmas tomorrow and at the goal and end of our days and of all days.

Christ, thou Lamb of God who didst bear the sins of the world, have mercy upon us, grant us thy peace. Amen.

Predigten 1954–1967, Zurich (1981), pp. 243ff., 247–251.

IV. The Gift of Freedom

"A little . . . "

A LITTLE HARDLY SUGGESTS WEALTH, yet it may often be much. One cannot put a label on those who have a little of many things. Barth saw no contradiction in having a little faith, a little Marx, a little laughter, a little seriousness. Christ, the royal man, espoused no single system or program; he teaches us the freedom of God's kingdom. Where others, then, might adopt "isms," Barth sought to be faithful only to God, not to human ideas. For him ideologies and principles were only illusory garments. He thought it better to be free with "a little" in the fullness of God's gift of freedom, than to put everything under a single label and finally have nothing.

At Safenwil on March 7, 1920, Barth preached on 2 Corinthians 2:14 – 17: "The Freedom of the Word of God."

We all have a natural desire, for example, that people should accept our character, that they should acknowledge us and delight in us as we are. To this end we all polish and smooth certain fatal points and corners in our wares lest these be too obvious. And unconsciously we are always concerned to advertise ourselves a bit so as to win approval for our valuable personality. And it gives us childish pleasure when we find those who will buy what we are. In the world the same is true even with the highest ideals. . . . With good reason, ideals are much valued merchandise. . . . Happy are those who have them to offer! But they must know how to do it, how to make them palatable and attractive. What we call "higher" must be presented in such a way that it does not seem to be something too special or unattainable but if possi-

ble simply a fruit of the natural instinct of self-preservation
that one may pluck only if this instinct is properly understood
and regulated. Christianity must be put in such a form that
people will say, "Oh yes, that is what we have always
thought and felt in our hearts." Political ideals must be set before people in such a way that they can see with joy and
astonishment how supreme righteousness and their own supreme interest happen to be one and the same. Look you, the
great, quiet secret of most great speakers, preachers, and
authors is this: They are outstanding salesmen who know
how to reach their customers and stir their desire to buy.
They are skilled in the art of bargaining and letting others bargain with them. For many great causes in the world, and for
most of the so-called spiritual and religious movements, what
counts is not so much that they are good or new or useful,
but that they have good salesmen who can achieve the
desired sales and find a satisfied public. This is how it is
done. Paul is not making any criticism when he says in the
text that this is how it is done. He merely wants to say that
you cannot do this with the Word of God. He merely wants
to point out that while there may be many good and not so
good things about which we may—and perhaps must—
bargain carefully, perhaps making various adjustments and
concessions, there is one thing that permits of no bargaining
and cannot be handled commercially. The Word of God is not
for sale, and therefore it needs no skillful salesmen. The
Word of God does not seek customers, and therefore we cannot hawk it or trade it, and it needs no middleman. The Word
of God does not compete with other articles that are on sale
at life's bargain counter. It is not ready to be sold at any price.
Its only demand is that it should simply be itself, that it
should not have to undergo any changes or adjustments, that
it should be allowed to shine in its own glory and thus be
snapped up by those who do not want to buy it but who will
accept it as grace, as a gift, just as it is.

Komm Schöpfer Geist! Predigten, Munich (1932), pp. 200–203 (ET Oxford [1978],
cf. pp. 216ff.).

On August 7, 1934, Barth spoke at a student conference at La Chataigneraie, Switzerland, on the theme "The Christian as Witness." In the discussion that followed he dealt with the objection that his view did not take real life into account.

Dear friends, do not think that I am speaking here as the advocate of a theoretical idea that I have worked out in my head. The words "abstract" and "theoretical" have been used. Believe me, I have had a little experience. I am a modern man, I belong to the age, I see its problems. You need not teach me so forcefully, perhaps, that life is what counts. No, I too have my practical life to live in this very stormy present, and I can tell you that it is precisely in life, wrestling with the modern world, that I have reached the path you heard about. I should perhaps describe the starting point before making my response to your criticisms. I was a pastor for ten years and had the task of preaching the gospel. I came up against the problem you all know well, that is, secularism, a modern world that finds a place for the church but follows different rules than the Christian rules we think we see in Holy Scripture. For some years this problem was in the forefront of all discussion. And I also found in this secularized Christian world a church or Christianity that for all its earnestness and zeal and inwardness and active and loving effort was much too closely related to this modern world. . . .

At every point it was no longer God's church, nor even tried to be. It was a church of pious people, of moral, good people, but still human. And I now maintain that this modern church is too closely related to the modern world. It is simply the reverse side of this world. This modern church and Christianity did and does what the world did when it liberated itself from God. There was a time in my life when this fact shocked me. I had taken the path you propose and tried everything on it that can be tried. And then one day I had a shock, for I found something different in the Bible, unlike the godlessness of the world and the godlessness of the church and Christianity. . . .

When I listen to you, I feel reminded of a period in Christian history some 200 years ago. At that time the church and Christianity thought they had to make the great discovery that you are suggesting to me: not just doctrine but life! Not just the word but love and deed! This was the age at the beginning of the eighteenth century, when Pietism rose up against the orthodoxy of the seventeenth and sixteenth centuries. Much of its criticism of the preceding period was right. From the Reformation onwards, the church had heard the message of God and Christ, but now, 150 years later, something was missing: the Christian life. There was preaching, good preaching, but love was not active. And at this moment, mark you, when people were shocked and distressed as they looked back on the Thirty Years War and the gloomy seventeenth century, they made the great mistake of *not* saying: We want to understand and to hear better, we want to let God be God and Christ be Christ in a new way, we want to tread very differently this path from baptism to the Lord's Supper. Instead, they thought that they *themselves* should make things better. They would cultivate the Christian life. They turned aside from God, and in very serious, worthy, and devout forms they began to cultivate what we now see before us in full bloom: pious Christians. But the honoring of piety slowly, yet logically, became the honoring of morality. And finally, when human piety and morality became so important, it became less important to speak about God, Christ, and the Holy Spirit, and people began to talk about human reason. . . . If we begin to take pious people as seriously as you wish, then, if we are not to be "one-sided," we will end up where the official German church is today. . . . Once you find a place for the self as well as God . . . there is no stopping. Be warned! Once you say, God *and* . . . , you open the door to demons. . . . We have experienced this in Germany. The only possible force that can meet the enemy and say no is the message that God is our *only* Helper.

Theologische Existenz heute 12, Munich (1934), pp. 25–28.

In Kaiserswerth on the evening of January 9, 1935, Barth spoke to some students on Psalm 16:1. He had just been suspended from his Bonn professorship for refusing to take the Hitler oath without the reservation: "So far as I can responsibly do so as an evangelical Christian."

"For I trust in thee." A remarkable "for." Does it mean that I acquire a claim by trusting? Certainly not. Who of us can come in that way to God and say, "Look, I have trusted in thee, and thou must protect me." If God had to protect us for that reason, it would go ill with us. The very reverse is true. Before God's face we always find that we have not trusted him and will not trust him. It is when we reach the point of admitting this that we can understand what the Bible means by the words, "For I trust in thee." It is saying that in God is my refuge. I cannot save myself. I flee. I do not know how to help myself. In Scripture, to trust in God is to know no place to go for help except to the living God himself, to be robbed of all supports and to flee to him. Among the supports of which we are robbed is our little bit of trust in God, our little bit of faith, our little bit of seriousness, our little bit of confessing. "I have no good apart from thee," the Psalm goes on to say. Don't you see that trust in God, true trust in God, begins where everything else ends? It begins when we realize that if there is salvation, comfort, or direction, it is not in me, or above me, or under me, but wholly and utterly in Jesus Christ my Lord, who has done it all for me. He, and he alone, provides it. If only we could understand this "he" as a "thou"—"I trust in *thee*"—then we would begin to understand the word "faith," which is so important in the Bible. Then we would also understand the saying, "For I trust in thee." It is not primarily a matter of our giving up everything, of our despairing, but of the glory of God arising for us as the glory whose light puts all else in shadow. All other things become small and insignificant for us as we realize that we cannot build on them. We thus take refuge in him. We pray to him not out of despair, but more truly out of simple joy. If everything else is taken from us, this means not an end, not destruction, but the light of grace shining over our lives and making us thankful.

"Das Evangelium in der Gegenwart," *Theologische Existenz heute* 25, Munich (1935).

In Zurich, on February 2, 1950, Barth gave a lecture on "Humanism." At the time he was at work on Church Dogmatics III, 1–4, *in which (III,2) he would find the basic form of humanity in the humanity of the man Jesus.*

Christian humanism is a contradiction in terms. Every attempt in this direction has proved it. We should avoid such attempts, for words ending in "ism" are of no real use in theology. They speak about systems and principles. They proclaim a world view or morality. They intimate the existence of a front or party. The gospel, however, is neither principle, system, world view, nor morality; it is spirit and life, the good news of God's presence and work in Jesus Christ. Nor does it form a front or party, not even in favor of a particular view of humanity; it builds up a community in the service of all humanity. The gospel is, of course, centrally concerned with humanity. But what it has to say about humanity, for it (also against it), and to it, begins at the point where the various humanisms break off, and breaks off at the point where they begin. In the light of it, one can understand what they are all saying and affirm and accept much of it. . . . But one must finally oppose them all for the very reason that they are humanisms, or abstract programs. Theology does not compete with them. It has nothing similar or comparable with which to oppose them. It can even adopt the term "humanism," although this was originally fashioned without it and even against it. But it can accept no responsibility for its definition. It cannot pretend to be surprised if its definition finally proves to be impracticable. Humanism smacks a little of ungodliness and idolatry.

Theologische Studien 28, Zollikon–Zurich (1950), p. 21f.

In May 1947, the journal unterwegs *(Berlin) published a discussion that Barth had led at Hamburg on August 5, 1947. The aim of the journal was church renewal along the lines of the Barmen Declaration of 1934.*

Question: Do not the fathers help us to find an answer? Answer: The situation is the same as with the confessions. The confessions should be an aid to our own theological reflection, dogmatics, and preaching. If I read the ancient prayers, it is not to pray them again, but to be led by them to prayer; then I myself pray, or I want the church of today to pray. I believe that fundamentally many things in them do not arise out of the needs of the kind of worship we should offer today. In their time the ancient prayers corresponded to such needs—I do not contest that—but now they represent a movement of escape, of escape from the present to the past.

For many years I myself have made it a part of sermon preparation to write an opening and closing prayer. In so doing I have had previous prayers in mind, but I want the congregation to pray with me here and now. What do I mean? Let me give an example. The ancient liturgies have a threefold *Kyrie*: "Lord, have mercy upon us." Is it not enough to pray this very sincerely just the once?

Do we not have to emphasize to pastors that their real task is to pray with their people? Then we can give them plenty of ancient texts, not to use, but to learn from.

"Brechen und Bauen . . . ," in K. Kupisch (ed.), *Der Götze wackelt*, Berlin (1961), pp. 117f.

In Church Dogmatics *III,4,* § *54,1, Barth gives an example of the way in which the freedom of obedience is true freedom, the freedom of the children of God.*

When a man hears the divine command, he simply cannot deny that, within the limits of the transgression of which it will constantly accuse him, but there in all seriousness, it discloses to him quite definite possibilities which he is well able to realize — small, individual, yet not contemptible possibilities. . . . In the one case it may be that more strictness, precision, and sobriety is demanded, in the other more patience and generosity; in the one case a certain discipline, in the other some degree of purification. That he should make use of such possibilities . . . is what is definitely required of a man who has heard the command as the command of Jesus Christ. If he refuses to do so, this means that . . . he has not really acknowledged it as a command, that he has probably not even heard it as such, and that he has not yet truly admitted the validity of its accusation. If he has done this, he will . . . make use of the possibility of relative amendment which it offers him. He need not fear that in so doing he will suddenly or gradually become a "saint," or be tempted to regard himself as such. The same command of God which summons him to this effort and equips him for it will unremittingly confront him with the One who alone pronounces and makes him free and righteous. . . . But the very same command which refers him to God's free grace, and therefore humbles him, restores and renews him against all frivolity, laziness, and resignation, continually directing him to the aims which are within the limits of his will and are therefore attainable. . . .

There is, for example, a certain orderliness and therefore integrity in the whole approach to the sexual question, a certain restraint in face of the tempting and recurrent phenomenon of erotic religion and religious eroticism, a certain healthy limitation of the dominance and exercise of the physical sexual impulse, a certain sovereignty in face of the question whether or not to marry, a fine naturalness with which a man may really be a man and a woman a woman, but also a fine naturalness with which each may recognize the other as such and behave accordingly, and a fine naturalness in which the order of the sexes may be manifested as such. All this exists. And if there is no perfect marriage, there are marriages which for all their imperfection can be and are maintained and carried through, and in the last resort not without promise and joyfulness . . . and fragmentarily, at least, undertaken in all sincerity as a work of free life-fellowship. There is also loyalty even in the midst of disloyalty and constancy amid open inconstancy. And . . . there is genuine, strong and wholehearted love even in relationships which cannot flower in regular marriage, but which in all their fragmentariness are not mere sin and shame. . . . All these things have, of course, their limits, their weaknesses and their serious problems. They certainly cannot stand in face of God's command. Measured by the latter, they are simply a heap of ruins. They can be good only on the basis of God's sinforgiving grace and within its limits. They can be regarded as relatively good only through faith. But we must not forget that the arch of the divine command spans the whole reality of this sphere and all who live therein. This means not only that there is here no one who is not struck by the divine judgment, but also that there is no one who is not reached by the divine mercy and in his own way held and comforted.

KD III, 4, Zurich (1969), pp. 267f. (ET *CD* III, 4, Edinburgh [1961]), pp. 238f.).

Concerned about the East–West conflict and the rearming of West Germany, Barth on May 25, 1952, gave a radio address on the question "What Shall We Do?"

I think especially that we should not be so afraid—of the wicked aims of others. Naturally we *can* be afraid in the modern world. But we can do many things that we *should* not do. To be afraid today is to want war, as the other side sees, whether its aims be good or bad, and then it will become afraid and want war too. Every day that we have some kind of peace, those who do not want war should be sure of their own cause—and of good courage. Those who do this, and do not act as though . . . the good Lord were dying and the other side would soon gobble us up, are doing their bit for world peace.

Second, those who are not going to be afraid must be people who are determined to see with their own eyes, hear with their own ears, and think with their own heads. They must not worry about being in a minority or even standing alone. They must not let themselves be made into a mass product by public opinion or propaganda. The organized and mobilized masses are always and everywhere the true danger to peace. Their outcry, however it may run, is false; it is secretly a war cry. What we need are free people who will march ahead through the outcry both right and left. Peace is threatened because there are so few of them.

Third, those who are not afraid but are free and peace loving will be open to the need and distress of their fellows and to the question of how they might help a little. They will be capable of not taking their own ideas with such deadly seriousness. Other people are important, not just I and my principles. War threatens because so many people have swallowed a ruler and go about with morose faces, making life hard for one another. Away with rulers! If we cannot sigh and laugh a little with others, we are warmongers even though we might be the greatest lovers of peace.

K. Kupisch (ed.), *Der Götze wackelt*, Berlin (1961), pp. 160f.

At Bielefeld, on September 21, 1953, Barth addressed the Society for Evangelical Theology on "The Gift of Freedom."

We begin by considering what we can know about God's own freedom. Do I have to justify myself if—here, and not elsewhere—I do not start off with the freedom that we are given? I have heard it rumored that we can speak about God only as we speak about ourselves. I do not dispute that. Properly understood, it makes the true point that God is not without us. In the present context, we have to see that God's own freedom is his freedom for us, so that we cannot speak about God's own freedom except with reference to the history between him and us, and we have to go on at once to speak about the freedom that we are given. But if this is to be properly understood, the thesis needs an antithesis: We can speak about ourselves only as we speak about God. It will then be beyond dispute among Christian theologians. But there is a difference of opinion whether the thesis comes first or its opposite. I myself am resolutely of the opinion that what I called the antithesis is the real thesis and should therefore come first. . . .

If God is for us the first reality, how can we ourselves be the first truth? Sometimes those who champion the opposite view make what is perhaps the overstrong statement that the freedom we are given by God is primarily a self-liberation. But if this is so, how, as thinkers, can we begin with ourselves? Is it so self-evident that we are from the very first known, but God is the great problematical unknown? Is it a law of the Medes and Persians that only on the basis of what we know about ourselves can we at best ask about God . . . ? How could we know that there is such a thing as freedom, or what it might be, if God had not come to us and shown us his own freedom as the source and norm of all freedom? We do not speculate about ourselves or abstract from ourselves and our own freedom. We seek and find concrete human freedom when we first ask about humanity's God and his freedom. . . .

In the freedom of his grace God is for us in every respect. He surrounds us on all sides. He is our Lord, before us, above us, after us, and in the history that is our existence, with us. In spite of our littleness, he is with us as our Creator, whose intentions and dealings with his creatures are perfectly good. In spite of our sin, he is with us as he who in Jesus Christ reconciled the world (and us with it) in gracious judgment, so that even our wicked past is not struck through as unfitting, but raised up to him. In spite of the corruption and transitoriness of our flesh, he is with us in our very being, present here and now through his Spirit as yesterday's Victor, present as power, summons, and comfort. In spite of our death, he is with us as the One who meets us on the frontier of the future as our Redeemer and Perfecter, setting the totality of our existence in the light which, in his eyes, has always been bright through every turning point. In this being and action of his with us, God inaugurates the history of our salvation.

Theologische Studien 39, Zollikon–Zurich (1953), pp. 2f., 5f.

In the summer of 1953, Barth began the lectures that formed the basis of Church Dogmatics *IV,2. In his portrayal of the man Jesus in § 64, he reminds us that Jesus was God's kingdom in person, and that as the royal man he effected a transvaluation of all values, his last word being for us and not against us.*

Jesus was not in any sense a reformer championing new orders against the old ones, contesting the old ones in order to replace them with the new ones. He did not align himself and his disciples with any of the existing parties. One of these, and not the worst, was that of the Pharisees. But Jesus did not identify himself with them. Nor did he set up against them an opposing party. He did not represent or defend or champion any program. . . . He was equally suspected and disliked by the representatives of all such programs, although he did not particularly attack any of them. Why his existence was so unsettling on every side was that he set all programs and principles in question. And he did this simply because he enjoyed and displayed . . . a remarkable freedom that again, we can only describe as royal. He had need of none of them in the sense of an absolute authority that was vitally necessary for him. . . . On the other hand, he had no need consistently to break any of them, to try to overthrow them altogether, to work for their replacement or amendment. He could live in these orders. He could seriously acknowledge in practice that the temple of God was in Jerusalem, and that the doctors of the law were to be found in this temple, and that their disciples, the scribes, were scattered throughout the land, with the Pharisees as their most zealous rivals. He could also acknowledge that the Romans were in the land with their native satellites, and that the emperor in Rome exercised supreme rule even over the land and people of the divine covenant. He could grant that there were families—and rich and poor. He never said that these things ought not to be. He did not oppose other "systems" to these. He did not make common cause with the Essene reforming movement. He simply revealed the limit and frontier of all these things— the freedom of the kingdom of God.

KD, IV, 2, Zurich (1985), pp. 191f. (ET *CD* IV, 2, Edinburgh [1958], pp. 171f.).

In Basel, on October 6, 1959, Barth took part in a discussion on the subject "Pietism and Theology." It arose out of his overtures to Pietism in Church Dogmatics *IV, 2 (KD, p. vii, CD, p. x); in it he tried to state his position in relation to it.*

When one is on the way from the seventy-third year of life to the seventy-fourth, one cannot count on having very much time left. My task, then, is to push on with the *Church Dogmatics* as far as I can. This is the real contribution that I can make. For the rest, "things will be better in heaven when I sing in the chorus of the blessed. . . . " My advice to you is that you drop the name Pietism. All words that end with "ism" are bad. Calvin-ism! I do not want to be called a Calvinist. Lutheranism is even worse. We should not espouse any "isms." Simply stand for an evangelical Christianity. Servants do not have to become "fathers." What counts is the person of Christ.

"Karl Barth und die Pietisten," *Monatsschrift Pastoraltheologie* 49, Göttingen (1960), p. 354.

For the main part of Church Dogmatics *IV, 4, Barth planned an exposition of the Lord's Prayer. After his death, the incomplete manuscript was published as* The Christian Life.

As only God himself can be at issue in the prayer of Christians for the coming of the kingdom, so only man can be at issue in their other thinking and speech and action. Man himself is he whom God loved, for whom Jesus died and rose again, and for whom he will come again as Judge and Redeemer. To him as such, Christians owe righteousness, their whole attention and concern, and mercy. They do not believe at all that clothes make the man. They cannot be impressed or deceived, then, by the Sunday clothes or working clothes or fool's clothes in which they will often enough meet him. They will not fear him because of the armor and cut-and-thrust weapons with which he tries to impress them and behind which he simply hides his anxiety, and they certainly will not despise him because his coat has too many holes to conceal effectively the emptiness of his vanity and his real need. They will not see him as political or economic or ecclesiastical man — the less so the more he claims to be a high priest or the like. They will not see him as the member of this or that country or sociological stratum, nor as the type of this or that psychological category, nor as one who believes in this or that doctrine of salvation or perdition. They will not see him as a good citizen or a convict, as the representative of a belief or party they find agreeable or painful, as a Christian or a non-Christian, as a good or bad, a practicing or nonpracticing Christian.

Das christliche Leben, Zurich (1979), p. 466 (ET Grand Rapids [1981], p. 269).

On June 21, 1968, Barth wrote to an engineer in East Germany in reply to a question about Christians and political parties.

But now to the question that has bothered you for a long time. Well, it is something of a surprise to me that you in East

Germany should be bothered by the fact that I belonged for a while to the Social Democratic Party. I believe that there is no real reason for this to concern you any longer. It sounds very fine and good that as a Christian one should not belong to any political party, but this is true only when it is a matter of belonging in principle. Being a Christian, however, is not just an inward and private matter. (In this regard we may calmly be taught a little and warned a little by Karl Marx.) Faith in God's revelation has nothing whatever to do with an ideology that glorifies the status quo. (Here again we should be bold and read Marx attentively.) Serious service of God should always include a political service of God. Christians cannot get by in some other and cheaper way. As Christians they must also make political decisions. This means that in specific cases, in relation to specific points and tasks, they can and should join up with a party that stands for the right thing.

In specific cases! When as a young parson in Safenwil in the Aargau, I saw the unjust situation of the workers, who were deprived of their rights, then I believed that as a theologian I could meet both them and the other members of the community only by taking their side and therefore becoming in practice a Social Democrat. In so doing, I was less interested in the ideological aspect of the party than in its organizing of unions. And "my" workers understood me on this matter. For them I was their "comrade parson" who was even ready on one occasion to march with them behind a red flag to Zofingen, just as they for their part were prepared (sometimes) to become zealous hearers of my sermons. . . . At times I even represented them at various congresses. Once I was almost elected to the Aargau council of government by the Socialists. Who knows, if I had not in the meantime found other and perhaps more important things to do, I might have ended my days as a famous Swiss politician!

The other time I had to consider supporting Social Democracy was shortly before the Nazis seized power. At that time my joining the party was above all a protest against the increasingly dangerous spread of the darkness of Hitlerism. In view of the way the Socialists were being restricted and contested at the time, and in view of the way they contradicted and resisted the rising Thousand Year Empire, I regarded it very simply as the right thing, quite apart from all other political motives, that I should accept solidarity with them as I did.

Today I am no longer a member of their party. . . . Without belonging to the party, however, I have constantly put in my little word, and still do so, that the walls and barriers to the East that have been put up so zealously and passionately in the West should be torn down. You will have heard this, and I hope it does not trouble you. It is also my serious hope that after these explanations you will no longer have any worries on this whole matter when you think of me.

Briefe 1961–1968, Zurich (1979), pp. 486ff. (ET Grand Rapids [1981], pp. 302ff.).

On April 7, 1968, in a radio interview, Barth explained what he meant by "liberal."

Let me begin by saying that when I call myself liberal, what I primarily understand by the term is an attitude of responsibility. For freedom is always a responsible thing. And that means further that I always have to be open—here we come, do we not, to what is usually meant by freedom? I might then add a third element. Being truly liberal means thinking and speaking in responsibility and openness on all sides . . . and with what I might call a total personal modesty. To be modest is not to be skeptical; it is to see that what one thinks and says also has its limits. This does not hinder me from saying very definitely what I think I see and know. But I can do this only with the awareness that there have been and are other people before me and alongside me, and that others still will come after me. This awareness gives me inner peace, so that I do not think I always have to be right even though I do say definitely what I say and think. Knowing that a limit is set for me, I can move cheerfully within it as a free man. Does that make sense . . . ?

One should be on guard against all words ending with "ism." Liberalism might also become an ideology—a rigid thing—and then it's no longer worth anything. In this sense, precisely as a liberal, I am free from liberalism. But the decisive point is to be free from oneself and not to regard oneself as the center of the world and the source of all truth. . . .

Question: To return to your socialism, if you will pardon another word ending in "ism." It is not to be supposed that you were a Marxist?

No, I was never that, decidedly not. What interested me about socialism in Safenwil was especially the union movement. I studied this for some time and helped it too, so that when I left Safenwil there were three flourishing unions where there had been none before. This was my modest involvement in the labor question and my very limited and for the most part practical interest in socialism. Naturally, I did other things too. But the doctrinaire or ideological aspects were always marginal for me.

Letzte Zeugnisse, Zurich (1970), pp. 35f., 40f., 44f. (ET Grand Rapids [1977] pp. 34f., 37, 39).

V. The Church as Watchman
"As though nothing had happened"

THE MIND OF A WISE MAN will know the time and way" (Eccl. 8:5). But how can we know the beginning and the end (3:11)? Is it not our lot to enjoy our work (3:22)? To the annoyance of both friend and foe, Barth knew how to be silent, and then how to speak when he had listened in silence. He understood it to be the church's watchman office always both to hear God's word and to proclaim it. What he wanted was to fear, love, and trust God above all things. He could be accused of engaging in a heavenly monologue when others were dumb in torment. He could sould like "a lonely bird on the housetop" (Ps. 102:7) "as though nothing had happened." In June 1933, however, he published Theologische Existenz heute in the midst of the church conflict and sent a copy to Hitler himself, noting that he could not answer Hitler's views directly because evangelical theology must go its own way unhampered. Some 37,000 copies of the pamphlet were printed before it was confiscated in July 1934._

In a way that I cannot finally ignore, I have been told that many of my former students and others who have shared in my theological work have long since been asking whether I do not have anything to say about the problems and concerns that have been troubling the church for some months. I might first point out that the decisive thing I am trying to say today about these problems and concerns is something I cannot make the subject of a special statement. This is because, in an apparently irrelevant and impalpable way, it consists very simply of the fact that in lectures and exercises with my students here in Bonn, now as earlier and as though nothing had happened—perhaps in a more emphatic tone but with no direct reference—I try to pursue theology and theology alone. In the same way the worship of the Benedictines in nearby Maria Laach will no doubt pursue its orderly course under the Third Reich without interruption or deviation. I believe that in this way I am taking up a position, at any rate an ecclesiastico-political position, and indirectly a political position as well.

Theologische Existenz heute, Munich (1933), p. 3 (ET Lexington [1962], cf. pp. 9f.).

The Bonn lectures of 1931 and 1932, which formed the basis of Church Dogmatics I, *show plainly that Barth regarded theological clarification as an essential prerequisite of political clarification (cf.* CD *I, 1, pp. xvf.).*

Theological thinking which by the grace of God is truly responsible and relevant, and stands in true connection with contemporary society, will even today show itself to be such by not allowing itself to be drawn into discussion of its basis, of the question of the existence of God or of revelation. On the contrary, it will refrain from attempted self-vindication as its theme demands, and thus show its responsibility and relevance by simply fulfilling itself as thinking on this basis, and therefore by simply existing as the witness of faith against unbelief. . . .

Thus it is precisely in terms of its origin and basis, of the being of the church, that church proclamation, and with it the church itself, is assailed and called in question. No other attack that may arise can even remotely harass the church in the same way as this one. To the degree that it is really harassed here it can and should be of good courage in face of all other assaults. But the harassment in this question will always have two aspects, the one relating to the past and the other to the future. . . . Between the yesterday and the tomorrow . . . there arises the question of the responsibility which is our present concern. Because it is God's service that church proclamation seeks to be, it is God himself and God alone who asks where and to whom response must be made here. But for this very reason . . . the church is seriously and concretely burdened with this responsibility. . . . If the church with its proclamation can feel secure before God, then other responsibilities will become burning ones, and it can and must happen that all the opposition to church proclamation from the standpoint of the state, society, culture and the like, though not intrinsically justifiable, will be legitimate in relation to the church, and will become very necessary criticism of the church in its whole failure to be the church. . . .

The church should fear God and not fear the world. But only if and as it fears God need it not fear the world. If it does not fear God, then it is not helped at all but genuinely endangered if it fears the world, listens to its opposition, considers its attitude, and accepts all kinds of responsibilities towards it, no matter how necessary and justified may be the criticism it receives from this quarter. . . .

It will always be a venture, a departure from its true line, when dogmatics thinks it should devote itself to this proclamation of God's word outside the church, or when, conversely, it thinks it should also speak to the world and not to the known visible church, which is its normal office. . . .

Theology has all too often tried to seek out and conquer the consciousness of an age on its own ground. We have protested already against theology allowing adversaries to dictate its action, since this can only mean conceding to them half or more than half of what should not be conceded, namely, the church's lack of independence over against the world and the primacy of the questions the world has to put to the church over the questions the church has to put to itself. Might it not be today that a theology which refuses even in method to make common cause with the aforesaid "humanizing of life" will be more relevant—if this is the point— than one which admits at the very outset that it can speak only a second word, a word on the situation (the situation outside the church)?

Kirchliche Dogmatik I, 1, Zurich (1985), pp. 28, 74f., 131 (ET Edinburgh [1975] pp. 29f., 73f., 81, 127f.).

Writing to former students in the Confessing Church on May 10, 1937, Barth added a Swiss voice to the German church conflict.

In itself, political decision is not Christian. In church proclamation it should never for a moment appear that this in itself and as such is the issue and not simply and solely obedience to the gospel. The church should never for a moment take the side of, and it should never for a moment think or act in agreement or union with, those for whom it is merely a matter of political decision as such. Now as always, the church must not engage in mere politics. I can see that today it is hard not to form a political opposition, just as four years ago it was very hard or impossible not to go along with the political stream. I think I can judge how hard it is to do the one thing and not the other. May you all have the wisdom you need to steer day by day between the two threatening cliffs of fear and recklessness, of sacral retreat and secular outburst, of blindness to political reality and political cleverness. I am glad that I may assume that in this matter there is between us a greater fundamental unity than there was four or even two years ago, when our unity was obviously somewhat obscured for a time.

In conclusion, may I say a few personal words? The main thing that I have to tell you is that the work you know so well goes ahead in all its details here in Basel . . . that we are trying to see to it that here at least in Europe, theology lives on "as though nothing had happened."

Theologische Existenz heute NF 49, Munich (1956), pp. 73f.

*On December 5, 1938, Barth drew up eight theses on "The Church
and the Political Question of Today." In this statement he described
anti-Semitism as "sin against the Holy Spirit" (p. 90).*

Actual confession takes the form of confessing, a specific
confession that is made here and now today. Confession in
this form deals necessarily with present-day questions that
agitate the church and the world. It does so not for the sake
of the questions or answers to them, but for the sake of the
present-day witness that must be borne to Jesus Christ. It
does so because this specific witness here and now, today,
can have form, tone, and color, and find vocal expression
only in its specific relation to the questions that agitate the
church and the world here and now, today. It certainly does
not do so in relationship—or at any rate in the same
relationship—to all the questions, not even all the so-called
burning questions, that agitate the church and the world. It
does so in relationship to the questions into whose sphere
and context it finds itself called by its own progress, by its
own inner necessity, in the responsibility which it owes not
to any situation, but in a given situation to the particular
leadership of the Lord of the church and to the particular witness of living Scripture. It always does so "as though nothing
had happened"—for here today, just as there yesterday, it
still has to bear witness only to Jesus Christ. But it does so always in light of what has actually happened. It does not
speak *to* the situation but *in* the situation; in the special situation chosen and characterized by itself, it speaks to the point.
It does not speak in terms of the spirit of the age, but to it and
with it, not because it fears or loves it but because this is the
spirit of the Jews and Gentiles (including Jews and Gentiles
in the church itself) who are meant to hear the gospel. . . .
     Undoubtedly, there are many questions that are not deci-
sive in confession, to which we neither can nor should say
yes or no. Perhaps not yet, perhaps no longer! The church is
in movement when making confession. To many present-day
questions it can and must be silent with its yes and no, perhaps provisionally, perhaps again as time and possibility

change. It must be silent when it finds no place to bear real witness to Jesus Christ, when it cannot present a yes or no that carries this witness. It is then best and safest to be silent about the questions at issue. The church should never merely reflect or discuss when making confession. This is not to deny but to affirm that in its confession the church must speak a decisive yes or no, must call white white and black black, when it finds time and opportunity to do so in witness to Jesus Christ. The time is not always ripe. It may be past, it may be still to come. But woe to the church if when the time does come it is silent, or merely reflects or discusses, or retreats into mere recitation. Woe to it if it sleeps, not just when great things are happening in the world . . . but when Jesus Christ himself is under assault and we ought to be watching with him. It is obviously only a short step from that to an open and conscious denial. On some questions the church that is confessing Jesus Christ must speak with a decisive yes or no. . . .

It is quite out of place when the church has to speak a yes or no and does not do so, or does so unclearly or weakly because it feels compromised by neighbors who are perhaps not wholly trustworthy and who are pronouncing the same yes or no. To make one's own cause serve another cause is one thing; to act in one's own cause and on one's own initiative because witness to Jesus Christ demands a yes or no is quite another.

Eine Schweizer Stimme 1938–1945, Zollikon–Zurich (1945), pp. 73f., 75f.

Barth spoke in various Swiss towns (January–February 1945) about a new beginning for postwar Germany based on Mathew 11:28. His position provoked strong attacks from German emigrés and some Swiss.

One thing is certain, that if the ghost of the swastika is laid to rest, the German eagle must go with it. One may doubt whether the German emigrés are clear about this. We must have no more German glory but, with extreme one-sidedness and difficulty, only German life. What is needed with everything else is the trust of other nations if a country is to have power, and even great or leading power. Germany has never enjoyed this trust; it does not enjoy it today. When it achieved power, it made a wrong and ultimately unsuccessful use of it. . . .

It is almost inconceivable, when all is over, how radically the Germans will be at an end and must begin again in every sphere. This time a long, a very long, convalescence awaits them. This time it will not be so easy to look back from a bad yesterday to a better day ahead. This time even the recollection of the undoubted bravery of the German army will not be able to put this war in a better light. This time no romantically motivated youth groups will go through the districts with guitars and songs as though nothing had happened, changing themselves on their return into the public menace of a warlike horde. This time German citizens and professors and students will not be able to return so quickly to the old paths. This time the greatest German solidity and eloquence will not be able to deceive the world so quickly. . . . The new Germany, no matter how things go, will be a land full of sorrow. . . . The German people will not disappear from the world's stage. But the stage has altered; inevitably its role will be a much more modest and wretched one. . . .

We shall find the end of the older Germany shattering if we will accept the insight that this end applies to us too, for it is a sign of the boundary that is immovably set not merely for the German way of life, both good and bad, but for the whole human way of life, including our own. It is a sign of the eternal law on which we shall break if we do not bow to it. . . .

How would it be if in the visible and obvious disturber of the peace, and the judgment that overtook him, we were to see ourselves—who are not such visible or obvious disturbers of the peace—and what at root we too have deserved . . . ?

Must we not respect the situation when, however justly, all the props have been knocked from under someone and the only option, under very painful circumstances and conditions, is to begin afresh, to make a completely new beginning? Might we not for a moment almost feel envy at this hopeless but incomparably fruitful situation? Only infrequently does a whole people have the chance to begin again at the beginning. . . .

No matter how bad things may be, the Germans will retreat into their shell if we approach them as teachers, and their young people will defend themselves with biting and scratching. They will think that those who come to them as teachers are against them, even more against them than those who previously came in airplanes and tanks. What the Germans need are friends, but real friends, and not like the friends of Job. . . .

Jesus Christ is for them, unconditionally for them. He is for them exactly as he is for us. He accepts the shame that covers us when he calls us his friends. If even for the best of reasons we resist and say that unconditional friendship for the Germans is too much to ask of us, then we must be careful lest the Savior's call, "Come to me, all who labor and are heavy laden," instead of passing through us, goes out to the Germans without applying to us at all. I recall once more the unique opportunity that they are given. How about if we were suddenly to read: "Come to me, you heartless ones, you wicked Hitler youth, you brutal SS soldiers, you vicious Gestapo villains, you sorry compromisers and collaborators, you mass men who for so long patiently and stupidly followed your so-called leader. Come to me, you guilty ones, you who share the guilt and who are now learning, and have to learn, what your deeds are worth. Come to me, I know you well, but I do not ask who you are or what you have done. I see only that you are at an end and for good or ill must begin again; I will refresh you, I will now begin again from the very beginning with you. If the Swiss, puffed up with their democratic, social, and Christian ideas, which they have always extolled, are not interested in you, I am. If they will not

say it, I will say it: I am for you, I am your friend."
Eine Schweizer Stimme 1938–1945, Zollikon–Zurich (1945), pp. 345f., 349, 351, 354f.

In Barmen on July 30, 1947, Barth gave a lecture on "The Message of God's Free Grace."

"To God alone be the glory" does not apply to any lofty idol or divine egoist or eternally morose deity, but to the "father of mercy and God of all comfort" (2 Cor. 1:3). It applies to one who has made it his glory to create and uphold the human race, to reconcile us to himself, to redeem and perfect us; to the One who has made our cause his own; to the One who has sought his holy divine right by giving us true human right under heaven and on earth. It applies to the One who has not swept aside our human needs, concerns, cares, distresses, and problems but taken them up, made them his own, and better than we can know or think answered and solved them. . . . Why does he want us to be free for him and therefore free from ourselves? So that we may be truly free. For the goal of the three last petitions of the Lord's Prayer, and of the six last commandments, is that grace may really be grace, the work and word of the one true God directed toward us and our human existence. . . .

Because it is free grace, the church's message cannot count on any human abilities, capacities, points of contact, or the like, or on any preparatory achievements or merits that might carry any weight. It is grace for creatures to whom God owes nothing. It is grace for sinners who have deserved only God's wrath. We do not possess it; it can only be imparted to us again and again. We experience it only as we constantly bow down and let it deal with us afresh as though we were nothing, as though nothing had happened. It confers itself without presupposition, reservation, or condition. We have it . . . only as we ask and pray and give thanks for it. . . . Only in this freedom is it demanding, sanctifying, costly grace. . . .

But let us never forget for a moment that in this freedom it is grace, addressed to us as we are, as weak creatures, as lost sinners, as those who walk in the shadow of death, but truly addressed to us. Grace means Immanuel—God with us. What was universally decided with the incarnation of God's Word, with the crucifixion and resurrection of Jesus Christ at the heart of history, was that we no longer belong to or are left to ourselves and our plight. Grace that does not ask what we are or have or bring, grace that leaves us no hope but in what we have not merited, God's free grace accepts us just as God's Word assumed flesh, our flesh, thus accepting us long before we could ever think of accepting it, comforting us already in life and in death long before we were ever aware of it, and irrespective of when or how we might become aware of it. God's grace goes out to us, and to be human means to be those to whom it has gone out. Jesus Christ would not be the Word by whom all things were made if we could escape this objective, ontic fact to which all our own decisions must refer. . . .

Jesus Christ remains, God remains, and with them the freedom of the church remains, its freedom for reformation after all the deformations of which it has been, and still is, guilty. God's free grace, which it may proclaim to all people, to the whole world, is its true portion and hope. This message that is entrusted to the church, even to the indolent and disobedient church, means that it always has . . . something original to say that people cannot hear elsewhere. . . . The unique and extraordinary thing about this message is imperishable, and this is what always makes the church free and forms the basis of its right and duty to exist. The message of the free grace of God also means that even when it falls asleep, the church cannot sleep too long. The message is like a trumpet that has the potential to arouse even in the hands of an unskilled player, to bring out from concealment, to make the church free again, to give it its proper place in the sun. The message means above all

that . . . the church can suddenly be present again, fashion-
ing free people . . . and in this sense free Christians, who
in spite of every secular or religious hindrance or entangle-
ment, venture at some point—as "the law of the Spirit of life"
commands (Rom. 8:2)—to begin again at the beginning as
though nothing had happened, and in the doctrine, life, and
order of the church and its relation to the world, defying
clergy, Pharisees, scribes, tyrants, the spirit of the age in politics, society, and science, and the great lord *Omnes*, to plow
a new furrow and not look back (Lk. 9:62).

Theologische Studien 23, Zollikon–Zurich (1947), pp. 5f., 18.

*Barth visited Hungary early in 1948 and concluded that the church
was adopting a good attitude toward the communist regime, avoid-
ing either radical opposition or collaboration. Emil Brunner in an
open letter accused him of relapsing from political activism into the
old message of 1933: "as though nothing had happened." Barth replied on June 6, 1948, arguing against any systematizing of political
history.*

I met responsible leaders of the Reformed Church in
Hungary, and I thought I should encourage them to tread a
narrow path between Moscow and Rome. I did not take a
ruler with me when I went, and so I left none behind. Their
past and situation and task are different from ours and from
those of German Evangelicals in the church conflict. If they
come to terms with their state and give themselves to the
church's own positive task, first and with all their power, this
is not the same as what the middle parties that you so much
valued, or even the German Christians, were doing in the
German church conflict. However that may be, it is, incidentally, an unfounded rumor that I was recommending "passive
unconcern" to the Germans in 1933 when I put it to them that
they should get on with the task of proclamation "as though
nothing had happened," that is, regardless of the supposed

revelation from God in Adolph Hitler. If they had done this consistently, they would have opposed to National Socialism a political factor of the first rank. For Hungary—and not for Hungary alone—everything depends on whether the church, bound not to principles but to its Lord, will seek and find its own way today, will learn how to choose freely the time to speak and the time to be silent, along with all the other times mentioned in Ecclesiastes 3, without being confused by any law that is not that of the gospel.

"Theologische Existenz 'heute.' Antwort an Emil Brunner," *Offene Briefe 1945–1968*, Zurich (1984), pp. 165f.

On a day of national mourning for the victims of the war and National Socialism, Barth gave an address at Wiesbaden (November 14, 1954) that provoked much protest because he also remembered those who fell in resistance movements (including communists) and he argued against the remilitarizing of West Germany.

We cannot forget ourselves. We were ourselves yesterday when we took part in these events, and if we are commanded to be different today, we must not forget what we were yesterday. . . . Even less can we forget the victims of the war and National Socialism. It is true that we escaped . . . but this does not mean that we can eat and drink and philosophize and politicize and dance on the graves of the victims "as though nothing had happened." Whether we knew and valued them or not, they were our neighbors, our human brothers and sisters. They were a part of us, and still are. They fell in a cause for which we are partly responsible. And they ask us, these victims of war, for what really did they fall and die and drown, for what did they suffer among us, sick and crippled. They ask us, these victims of National Socialism, where we were when they were murdered, and what we did that things came to such a pass. They ask us, these victims of the resistance movement, whether it was right for us to escape, why we did not have to take their path, why we did not really resist too. They themselves are in the hand of God, who knows the least as well as the greatest, their opinions and desires and sufferings, who still knows them, who has not forgotten and will not forget. But it would be totally unworthy if we were to forget them and repulse their questions. It would also be impossible; we cannot escape them.

Junge Kirche 15 (1954), p. 569.

On July 27, 1961, in the Hamburg journal konkret, *Barth answered the question of whether the movement against nuclear arms for West Germany was useless, because unsuccessful.*

The movement is certainly not meaningless but highly meaningful. There has been no lack of clear explanation or lively appeal with you or with us. But in both cases the people have reacted with indifference. Can we be surprised, then, that those who rule us, whether directly or indirectly, are going on with their evil designs "as though nothing had happened"? I am reminded of what happened in 1933, when it was the people—having eyes but seeing not—that first ignored Hitlerism and then had to put up with it. What they will have to put up with this time if they stupidly accept the atom bomb might well be final. Be that as it may, your group will also perhaps have to face the unmistakable fact that it is the fate of significant movements to be unsuccessful, that they must be ventured just the same, and that it is only when swimming hopelessly against the stream that one can really live—really, that is, "concretely."

Briefe 1961–1968, Zurich (1979), p. 16 (ET Grand Rapids [1981], p. 14).

In his 1958–1959 lectures, Barth delivered the material that went into Church Dogmatics *IV, 3. In § 73 ("The Holy Spirit and Christian Hope") he laid an ethical foundation in the subsection "Life in Hope."*

There have to be in the world men who even in the night, perhaps only at midnight or before, or possibly in the hour of early dawn, look forward to the morning, to the rising sooner or later of the Sun of righteousness, to the end and goal of all things and therefore to their own new beginning in light, which no further end can follow. There have to be men by whose irrepressible and constant unrest at least a few and perhaps even quite a number of their fellows are prevented from falling asleep as though nothing had happened and nothing out of the ordinary could happen in the future. In so doing they do provisionally . . . that which he himself will finally do with unequivocal and irresistible power when his day comes. To this extent they are his representatives. Yet in the act of hope we can and should also understand and describe Christians as on the other side representatives of the surrounding humanity which seems for the most part to slumber. One day the whole of the human race must awaken, not of its own volition or resolve, nor in consequence of the clamour and tumult of great catastrophes, but as the trumpet is sounded which no one, not even the Christian, can now blow, but which one day will be blown in such a way that neither the church nor the world can fail to hear it. The Christian now can only wake up for others, for the sleeping church and world around. He can only appear to them . . . as a watchman. Provisionally the church and the world hope in him as their representative. To this extent, even though he may be an isolated figure, he is a representative on this side as well.

Kirchliche Dogmatik IV, 3, Zurich (1979), pp. 1071f. (ET Edinburgh [1962], pp. 933f.).

VI. Pastoral Care

"Go with them in a relaxed and cheerful manner . . . "

*B*ARTH ONCE SAID OF A COLLEAGUE *that he was always worrying about who was greatest in the kingdom of heaven. He himself had no such worry. He could often laugh at himself and for this reason could also fight when the cause demanded. He was a complex person: tender and gruff, cheerful and pugnacious, open and reserved, questioning and confident, modest but with a strong sense of individuality. He became milder with age. As teacher, preacher, counselor, friend, and father, he tried to go with all who trusted him in a relaxed and cheerful manner as a fellow pilgrim whose final trust was in God.*

In 1948, Barth wrote an essay for The Christian Century *on how his mind had changed during the previous ten years. In Basel he wrote a second account in October 1948.*

At this age one's limits become clearer; this is one of the good changes in my life during the last ten years. Thus to my own surprise, and that of those who knew me earlier, I have become unmistakably milder, and even more peaceable, readier to see that one might be in the same boat even with opponents, ready to allow that I might at times be wrongly attacked without rushing to my own defense, and thus not taking such pleasure in attacking others. Saying yes now seems to me to be far more important than saying no, and in theology the message of God's grace seems much more urgent than the message—not to be suppressed—of God's law, wrath, accusation, and judgment. Signs of weakness? Perhaps. But on the one side I can still lay about me when I must. And on the other side I think I see that in this other form,

which is perhaps connected with my age, I have done more and could achieve more than in the bellicosity of earlier years.
Evangelische Theologie 8, Munich (1948–49), p. 276.

In Hungary, at the end of March 1948, Barth gave an address on "Modern Youth, Its Legacy and Responsibility."

Long live liberty! If modern youth wants to be free, it must be free to test its legacy, which has not simply vanished, and to honor and bring to new honor what is worth honoring in it. Much but not all was necessarily consumed by the fire and neither may nor should return. Some still waits for understanding eyes and ears and loyal hands.

That two and two make four, not five, was and is a precious truth, and must remain so in the coming age for which you are responsible. The Ten Commandments (Ex. 20:2–17) are also valid, or must reassume their validity after such a great outbreak of transgression. The serpent's plea that we should do evil that good may come must also be banned in the future. Lying must still be called lying in the future, and wrong wrong. Nor is it to be doubted that God will still be God in the future, and that as he has always done he will know how to find and judge those who would have it otherwise.

In the past there have always been those who could think independently and wanted to do so. It would not be good if there were none such in your generation. Listen to a few words from Immanuel Kant in his work "What is Enlightenment?": "Immaturity is the inability to use one's own understanding without guidance from another. This immaturity is culpable if it is not due to lack of understanding but to lack of the resolution and courage to use it without outside guidance. . . ." It would be good if the second half of the twentieth century, after the first half has unexpectedly brought with it so much sinister madness, could be in the best sense a time of such "enlightenment." It will be your job to see to it.

The future age, your age, will be, we hope, an age when the music of Mozart and the poetry of Goethe will find not less receptive but more well-tuned ears and more open hearts.

I do not think it can be a good age if there is no place in it for a constitutional federation (like the Swiss republic) that is freely formed and freely based on the will of the people.

Above all, it cannot be a good age if the gospel of Jesus Christ, the message of free grace, the word of the Christ who is Lord of all things and yet in love their servant, is silent and no longer to be heard in it.

My friends, you may have received the impression that I am speaking to you in praise of the past. It is my serious opinion that everything that is before us is more or less stained, weakened, and devalued. But the freedom of today's youth must show itself in acceptance of what was once true and right and good and beautiful, and especially in daring to discover, recognize, and confess afresh, even if in obscure form, what is eternal—and all this better than we have done. Do not in any case waste your inheritance, no matter how unattractive it may seem. One day you will have to pass it on to those who come after you. Perhaps you will think of me when those who are as yet unborn are before you and ask you what you have made of what is entrusted to your responsibility—to increase, not to diminish—in this time of great stress but also in such great freedom.

I draw to a close. If your freedom is to be genuine and strong, it must have a basis. What was called freedom in Europe's past has collapsed, and had to collapse, because at a secret depth, not just in wicked secular form but in moral and religious form, it had long since been a freedom for ungodliness and inhumanity. Describe and treat as a reactionary anyone who tries to commend this freedom to you under any title. Freedom is freedom for God and for others. Where it is anything else, it is not freedom for responsibility. In freedom for God and for others you will find the right words and take the right steps and grow to maturity in defiance of the idols of yesterday and today. You cannot then be doctrinaire, whether conservative, revolutionary, or even democratic. The New Testament describes this freedom as the freedom of the children of God, our freedom in Jesus Christ. Why? Because Jesus Christ as true God and true man has brought God and man together. "If the Son shall make you free, you shall be free indeed." This word was spoken to our generation. We did not really grasp it. Will it be given to your generation to grasp it better? May it be thus given! What is certain is that all of us, old and young, belong together as hearers of this word.

Christliche Gemeinde im Wechsel der Staatsordnungen, Zurich (1948), pp. 12–14.

On the evening of October 7, 1956, Barth preached in the Bruderholz chapel on Leviticus 26:12. The "trams" he mentions are the ones he used from his home to the university.

God is not immobile. He is not a rigid being. He is not a kind of prisoner of his own eternity. No, God is on the march. He comes and goes. He is the hero of a history. God moves; he is the living God.

"Among you," we read. The places where God moves, coming and going as the living God, are the streets on which we walk, on which the cars roll as well as the 15 and 16 trams, on which we go our different ways. His places are our houses with their dining rooms, living rooms, bedrooms, and kitchens, our gardens, our places of work, our places of amusement, and certainly also the Zwingli house, and why not this Bruderholz chapel? God is not absent, not in a different place from us. If he lives in heaven, he lives also on earth, in Basel, on the Bruderholz, among us and with us. He is always and everywhere the God who is near. He is not on the margin. He is nearer to us than we are to ourselves. He knows us better than we know ourselves. He deals with us better than we could do even with the best will and under-

standing. This is how he moves among us. For all the differences of people and their situations, he is the one God for each and all, now in this way, now in that. . . . God is the only true helper and supporter. One might put it thus: He wills to be the one who with divine seriousness and perfection says yes to us. His yes is a holy and salutary yes. It includes a no, a no to everything around us and in us that he must say no to for his own sake and ours. He is like a doctor who can and must give us medicines and pills to swallow that we do not like swallowing . . . who may send us to the hospital, which we do not enjoy . . . or who may demand a small or large operation—not pleasant but very necessary and helpful. Thus it is with God's yes and the included no, which we will not like. The fact remains that God is the one who with his no says yes to us—a full, unrestricted yes with no question marks, a yes pregnant with God's will and power to save us, to carry us, to set us on our feet, to make us free and merry. This means: "I will be your God." In short, and very simply: "I will be your *good*"—your good against everything evil, your salvation against all destruction, your peace against all strife. Moving among you, I will be your God."
Predigten 1954–1967, Zurich (1981), pp. 57f., 60.

Asked to say a word when hail devastated much of the grape harvest in a certain village, Barth replied in a letter dated November 17, 1958.

Many things like this hail occur in the world: wasting sickness, famine, accidents in mine and mountain, floods. . . . God's good creation shows two faces, the one bright and cheerful, the other gloomy and sad.

What is certain is that God, the author of this order, has not hesitated to share our human lot in Jesus Christ, and above all to share our sorrows. Those who suffer do not suffer without him but with him. What we suffer from the hail cannot be greater than what he suffered on Golgotha.

Why this order of things? Why the ambivalence of creation? Perhaps so that the world as it is might be a parable of salvation on the one side, that is, eternal glory, and the abyss on the other side, that is, the darkness and destruction to which we would be condemned had not Christ's resurrection assured us of the contrary.

Again, why? Perhaps to make it clear that we have no claim to the good things that life offers: good weather, good harvests, good grapes, good wine. Were we grateful for what was given us in good years for no merit of ours but by the sheer grace of the Creator?

Even more so, are we grateful for the eternal salvation that is given us in Jesus Christ by God's free decision? We should consider human ingratitude. It might be more relevant to document this, no matter how dreadful the hail is, as it undoubtedly is.

Offene Briefe 1945–1968, Zurich (1984), pp. 568f.

At the end of October 1958 (in a Basel hospital), Barth contributed this greeting to a festschrift for the physician Richard Siebeck.

Was it from the very outset the distinctive orientation of your medical work that made possible and necessary so much participation in theology? Or, conversely, was it because theology was so much on your heart that you were pushed in this direction as a physician? However that may be, the fruitful picture of the physician as one who, bending over patients, lends them assistance in full humanity, characterized both inwardly and outwardly all your medical work. . . . One might regard this picture as just as much an indispensable principle of concrete, theologically grounded ethics as it is of medical theory and practice. How far it has been accepted by either theologians or physicians is another matter. The crisis in medicine and theology that so agitated us at its onset some forty years ago has not been overcome in spite of all that we and others have attempted. And if to this day it is not easy to be a theologian along the lines then followed, I can imagine that in another way it must be especially hard to bring medicine into conformity with your picture and to keep it there. . . . Yet we can be sure of the goodness, not of our intention or achievement, but of the cause that stirs us, even if we see little or nothing of the success of what we are doing. You were and are for me a model inasmuch as I have never heard you speak of your work except with a determination that does not exclude but includes great modesty and restraint in every respect. There are so many secretly and openly arrogant theologians—and doctors too—and they are hardly those who know best what they want, because they want what they must. That is how it is with you. When people are sure of their cause, they can take pleasure in the thought that others will come after them to do things much better, and they can hope for a long life to see them at work. They can also rejoice already in the final revelation that will bring to light what is good, less good, and bad in our work, to our comfort and our shame, but in any case to our liberation and salvation.

Offene Briefe 1945-1968, Zurich (1984), pp. 447-449.

On December 27, 1959, Barth preached in Basel prison on Isaiah 54:10.

Have we not already considered that the surest thing one can have is a firm inner attitude and character, and a solid faith? These are undoubtedly good. Yet "let anyone who thinks that he stands take heed lest he fall" (1 Cor. 10:12).

Dear friends, there can be no question that fundamentally we all live on the edge of an abyss and that it is dreadfully easy to fall into evil, folly, and wickedness in thought, word, and act. This is true even when we are really trying to be Christians. Temptation has often come unsought to many good people. No, we cannot really believe in our character, in the good in ourselves. To do so can only have a bad outcome. We can and should believe only in what God is for us. We can and should believe only that Jesus Christ died and rose again for us. Christ's "blood and righteousness"—they alone—are our "beauty and flaming dress." I may be strong or weak, I may stand or fall, I may doubt or be confident, I may go my way in the dark or the light, but "my grace shall not depart from you"—cling to that, we all have to cling to that.

Predigten 1954–1967, Zurich (1981), p. 161.

Barth wrote this letter to a prisoner in Germany on December 20, 1961.

Since you obviously want something from me, you cannot be serious in expecting me to judge you harshly. But can I give you any supporting counsel?

You say you plunge deeply into the Bible in vain. You say you also pray in vain. You are clearly thinking of a "final step," but you shrink back from it. Have I understood you correctly?

First, regarding your prayers. How do you know they are in vain? God has his own time, and he may well know the right moment to lift the double shadow that now lies over your life. Therefore, do not stop praying.

It could also be that he will answer you in a very different way from what you have in mind in your prayers. Hold unshakably fast to one thing. He loves you even as the one you now are. . . . And listen closely: it might well be that he will not lift this shadow from you, possibly will never do so your whole life, just because from all eternity he has appointed you to be his friend as he is yours, just because he wants you as the man whose only option is to love him in return and give him alone the glory there in the depths from which he will not raise you.

Get me right: I am not saying that this has to be so. . . . But I see and know that there are shadows in the lives of all of us . . . which will not disperse, and which perhaps in God's will must not disperse, so that we may be held in the place where, as those who are loved by God, we can only love him back and praise him.

Thus, even if this is his mind and will for you, in no case must you think of that final step. May your hope not be a tiny flame but a big and strong one even then . . . for what God chooses for us children of men is always the best.

Can you follow me? Perhaps you can if you read the Christmas story in Luke's Gospel, not deeply but very simply, with the thought that every word there — and every word in Psalm 23 too — is also meant for you, and especially for you.
Briefe 1961–1968, Zurich (1979), pp. 35–37 (ET Grand Rapids [1981], pp. 27f.).

In the summer of 1966, Barth drew up these rules for older people in relation to younger.

1. Realize that younger people of both sexes, whether relatives or close in other ways, have a right to go their own ways according to their own (and not your) principles, ideas, and desires, to gain their own experience, and to find happiness in their own (and not your) fashion.

2. Do not force upon them, then, your own example or wisdom or inclinations or favors.

3. Do not bind them in any way to yourself or put them under any obligation.

4. Do not be surprised or annoyed or upset if you necessarily find that they have no time, or little time, for you, that . . . you sometimes inconvenience or bore them, and that they casually ignore you and your counsel.

5. When they act in this way, remember penitently that

in your own youth you perhaps (or probably) also acted in the same way toward the older authorities of the time.

6. Be grateful for every proof of genuine notice and serious confidence they show you, but do not expect or demand such proofs.

7. Never under any circumstances give them up, but even as you let them go their own way, go with them in a relaxed and cheerful manner, trusting that God will do what is best for them, and always supporting and praying for them.

Eine späte Freundschaft in Briefen, Zurich (1981), pp. 56f. (ET Grand Rapids [1982] p. 48).

On January 18, 1969, at a gathering for the world week of prayer in Zurich, Barth was to give an address on "Starting Out, Turning Round, and Confessing," but he died on December 10, 1968, leaving the manuscript unfinished in mid-sentence.

The church's true and authentic starting out takes place only when it sees the new as promise and therefore as future, as clear and definite promise and future.' Some years ago a young man in a gathering of clergy startled me by saying, "Professor, you have made history, but you have now become history. We young folk are setting out for new shores." I replied, "That is good. I am glad to hear it. Tell me something about these new shores." Unfortunately, he had nothing to tell. . . . In the church today there are many likable young pastors and priests who tell us very loudly that almost everything must be changed. If only God would tell them, or if they would let God tell them, and if they would then tell others, what is to replace the present setup, then and only then would their activity have something authentically and credibly to do with the starting out of the church.

Letzte Zeugnisse, Zurich (1970), pp. 65f. (ET Grand Rapids [1977], p. 56).

VII. The Overcoming of Evil
"Mephistopheles is absent"

DEATH MEETS US IN A THOUSAND FORMS. *It casts its shadow upon life and limits our love and hope. It seems to some as though its iron law applies even to God himself. But Barth rejected this false conclusion as folly. He would rather regard himself as dead than God. It would be stupid to deny that evil is at work in the world, but to think that it can contest God's place is to make hell the seat of the world's government. Mephistopheles is absent because evil is a defeated power. It does not rule and has no claim over us. Its defeat is not our business. Our business is to be thankful to God for giving his Son. We achieve true relevance when in faith, love, and hope we relate ourselves constantly to the fact that Jesus Christ is Victor.*

On October 6, 1957, at an evening service in the Bruderholz chapel, Barth preached on 1 Timothy 4:4f.

Bad, ugly, evil, and dangerous things exist. The world is full of them. But what is bad was certainly not created by God. It is the nature of what is bad, ugly, and evil not to have been willed or created by God. It may be known because it has nothing whatever to do with Jesus Christ and his grace. It serves neither God nor us. It is alien to the structure and meaning of the Father's house. It can come forth only from our corrupt hearts and understandings. It can derive only from the devil, who is not a second creator. Being rejected and denied by God, and set on his left hand, it is something that we can reject, avoid, fear, and flee, and that we are indeed commanded to avoid and flee. The fact that there are

90

bad things—many, many bad things—does not alter the truth that God's creation is good. Neither we nor the devil can alter this.

Predigten 1954–1967, Zurich (1981), p. 92.

In the Church Dogmatics *there are many allusions to Mozart and his music. In this music Barth found an objectivity corresponding to God's free grace, and he paid a notable tribute to it in Vol. III, 3.*

Mozart neither needed nor desired to express or represent himself, his vitality, sorrow, piety, or any program. He was remarkably free from the mania for self-expression. He simply offered himself as the agent by which little bits of horn, metal and catgut could serve as the voices of creation. . . . He made use of instruments ranging from the piano and violin, through the horn and clarinet, down to the venerable bassoon, with the human voice somewhere among them. . . . He drew music from them all, expressing even human emotions in the service of this music, and not vice versa. He himself was only an ear for this music, and its mediator to other ears. He died when according to the worldly wise his life-work was only ripening to its true fulfilment. But who shall say that after the *Magic Flute*, the *Clarinet Concerto* of October 1791, and the *Requiem*, it was not already fulfilled? Was not the whole of his achievement implicit in his works at the age of sixteen or eighteen? Is it not heard in what has come down to us from the very young Mozart? He died in misery like an "unknown soldier," and with Calvin, and Moses in the Bible, he has no known grave. But what does this matter? What does a grave matter when a life is permitted simply and unpretentiously and therefore serenely, authentically and impressively, to express the good creation of God, which also includes the limitation and end of man?

Kirchliche Dogmatik III, 3, Zurich (1979), p. 338 (ET Edinburgh [1960], pp. 298f.).

In Church Dogmatics *III, 4, Barth discussed the problem of relaxation in work.*

If man's work is to be done aright, relaxation is required. . . . Work under tension is diseased and evil work which resists God and destroys man. It is done under tension, however, when man does not rise above it but is possessed, controlled and impelled by it. This possession, control and impulsion obtain when he posits himself absolutely as the subject of the active confirmation of his existence. . . . He can and should affirm his existence actively, but only on the presupposition and in relation to the fact that it is already affirmed by his Creator who is his primary and true Lord. . . . He has simply to affirm his existence in creaturely and not divine activity. . . . That which he has been commissioned to do as a witness of the divine work is hard and strenuous enough. But he has not been commissioned to exercise the initiating and consummating function of God. He can and should leave this wholly to God. The demanded rest from all his labour is that he should do his work with diligence but also with the recollection that God is Lord, Master, Provider, Warrior, Victor, Author and Finisher, and therefore with the relief and relaxation which spring from this recognition.

To work tensely is to do so in self-exaltation and forgetfulness of God. All the faithfulness, zeal, conscientiousness and good intentions which a man may bring to this work do not alter the fact that in it he sins. . . . In it the fellow-humanity of right work is also forgotten and lost. The understanding of genuine and justifiable claims is also confused and man falls victim to empty and inordinate desires. He usually omits to investigate the difference between meaningful and meaningless aims. And he certainly cannot work objectively. Tension makes work a drudgery, a mad race, an affliction, not only for the worker but also for those around. He may and should work, but if he does so in a feverish state of tension everything goes wrong, he throws everything into confusion and he thus upsets himself and everyone else. This

should not be. We often think there is no other way. . . .
We are always mistaken if we think there is no option but to
work tensely. We should let ourselves be released from this
compulsion.

Such release ought to be regarded as a divinely ordained
hygiene . . . primarily in the sphere of outward work, but
also in that of inward as well. For there is a kind of reflection,
or self-preoccupation, of spiritual preparation, mobilization
and planning for all sorts of decisions, acts and works, which
has long since ceased to be orderly inward work. As a fruit-
less and restless revolving around a partly or wholly imagi-
nary impulse, it has become a spiritual tension . . . from
which we can and should be released by the simple reminder
that God is in charge. Rest in work does not mean taking
things easily, or being indifferent and careless. It simply implies relaxation in the execution of this work by an applied
knowledge of God and oneself. . . . Rest in work means
that even as he performs it man remains free in relation to it,
and above all in relation to himself.

Outward and inward work will be done with more rather
than less seriousness once a man realizes that what he desires
and does and achieves thereby, when measured by the work
of God which it may attest, cannot be anything but play, that
is, a childlike imitation and reflection of the fatherly action of
God which as such is true and proper action. When children
play properly, of course, they do so with supreme seriousness and devotion. . . . We are summoned to play
properly. But we must not imagine that what we desire and
are able to do is more than play. Human work would certainly not be worse done, but . . . much better, if it were
not done with the frightful seriousness which is so often be-
stowed upon it just because fundamentally we do not think
that we have to take God seriously, and therefore we must
take ourselves the more terribly seriously, this usually being
the surest way to invoke the spirit of idleness and sloth by
way of compensation. . . . Not by a long chalk can work be
done with genuine earnestness in these circumstances—and
this for the simple reason that we will not admit that in it,

even at best, we cannot be more than children engaged in serious and true play.

No type of work is exempt from this rule. It may be seen clearly in the work of the artist, since there it belongs to the very heart of the matter. Yet we might just as well be prepared frankly to admit its validity in scientific work as well. *Kirchliche Dogmatik* III, 4, Zurich (1969), pp. 633–636 (ET Edinburgh [1961], pp. 552–554).

On January 29, 1956, to mark the 200th anniversary of Mozart's birth, Barth gave an address on "Mozart's Freedom."

Let me say a word about what I might call the great objectivity with which Mozart went his way. . . . He sought and found in the natural and spiritual world only the occasions, materials, and tasks of his music. With God, world, humanity, self, heaven, earth, life, and especially death before his eyes and in his ears, he was profoundly simple and therefore free in a way that seems to have been permitted and obviously commanded him, and that is thus exemplary. This means that his music is also uncommonly free from all exaggerations, from all breaks and antitheses in principle. The sun shines, but it does not blind or consume or burn. Heaven arches over earth, but it does not weigh on it or oppress it or swallow it up. The earth is still the earth, then, but it does not have to assert itself in a titanic revolt against heaven. Darkness, chaos, death, and hell may be noted, but never for a moment do they gain the upper hand. As Mozart makes music, he knows all this from some mysterious center, and he thus observes the limits both right and left, both above and below. He maintains due proportion. . . . There is in his music no light that does not also know shadow, no joy that does not include pain, but also no terror, anger, or complaint that peace does not accompany either closely or at a distance. No laughter without tears, but also no tears without laughter . . . ! It is the absence of all demons, the refraining from extremes, the wise juxtaposition and mixing of elements, that constitutes the freedom with which in Mozart's music the true voice of humanity comes to expression in all its range— unstifled yet undistorted and free from tension. Those who hear it aright . . . understand themselves as the people they are . . . as those who have fallen victim to death but who still live, and they feel themselves summoned to freedom.

Wolfgang Amadeus Mozart 1756–1956, Zurich (1982), pp. 36, 39–41 (ET Grand Rapids [1986]).

On August 15, 1967, Barth wrote this letter to his new friend Carl Zuckmayer, with whom he shared a cheerful confidence in God's good creation grounded in God himself.

Since the beautiful 28th of July, when I visited your house with members of my family, you have heard nothing directly from me. That day was the high point of my stay (perhaps the last) in the Valais mountains. And the high point of that high point was undoubtedly the private conversation that I had with you. Rarely have I found a personal meeting so delightful as the unexpected one I had with you. . . .

Thanks for everything, but especially for the works, previously unknown to me, among which the volume of stories has made the deepest impression. . . . All of them in their different ways have moved me deeply, and, if I know myself, and you as the author, they have done so . . . in the never-failing compassion with which it is constantly given you to view human darkness, corruption, and misery. Mephistopheles is absent. In you the goodness of God that unobtrusively but unmistakably embraces all things and people governs and characterizes even the most trivial, bizarre, and foolish of scenes and situations. And the best is that you yourself hardly notice how much in what one might call your purely "secular" writings you have in fact discharged, and still discharge, a priestly office, and do so to a degree that is granted to few professional priests, preachers, and theologians, either Roman or Evangelical. I will not say anything about your poetic art, for I do not feel competent to do this. But as a layman in the field I may admit to you . . . that from the standpoint of your content, I regard you as a poet of the first rank.

Since we came to speak about predestination in our discussion at Saas-Fee, I have since had my publishers send you one of the many volumes of my dogmatics in which I have dealt specifically with this subject. I might well wonder whether you will be able to make anything of this specimen of academic Evangelical theology. If not, I shall not take it amiss. To make it easier, perhaps, I am having sent a little book of sermons preached in the prison here, in which you will possibly see more clearly how I have tried to bring the same statement that is made in the big volume to the simple man, or not so simple in this case, and above all have tried to pray with this man. . . .

I greet you as a friend, or rather as a younger brother, whom I found only late but with all the greater gratitude. . . . How lovingly and festively you welcomed our group that day in July.

Carl Zuckmayer, *Eine späte Freundschaft*, Zurich (1981), pp. 16–18 (ET Grand Rapids [1982], pp. 8f.).

Barth closed his evening sermon of October 6, 1957, with this prayer.

Lord, in thy great mercy thou hast given us life and all that we possess, and hast preserved them to this day. Forgive all the self-will and negligence and misuse of which we have always been guilty, even in the week that is past and on this Sunday. Do not let us fall either today or tomorrow. Free us from all tension or mere routine, and from the tyranny of custom, fashion, and public opinion. Let us hear thy word, and give us the courage and freedom to pray to thee. And so convert us continually to thanksgiving in heart and deed, that we may not perish but have everlasting life.

Do this work of thy good Holy Spirit also among all people, both near and far: in both small and great, in those with broader and those with narrower responsibilities and tasks, in employers and employees, in the healthy and the sick, in the wealthy and the needy, in those who must resolve and command and in those who must obey, in court officials and judges and in those who offend and are punished, in pastors and missionaries, in Christians and the non-Christians whom we may serve and want to serve.

Lord, have mercy upon us, thy people, thy creation. We laud and praise thee, for we know that thy mercy has no end and thy power no limits . . . Amen.

Predigten 1954–1967, Zurich (1981), p. 96.

VIII. Humanity before God

"Ah yes"

O LORD" IS A COMMON BIBLICAL complaint
and plea (cf. Ps. 3:2; Dan. 9:19; Amos 7:2), and "Yes, Lord" is
Peter's answer to Jesus when asked whether he loves him (Jn.
21:15ff.). Barth's sigh "Ah yes" rests on these biblical experiences.
It is a sigh for the world that does not yet know God's grace in
Christ. It goes to the heart of his theological work and is for him the
source of all prayer. It marks the life of those who, waiting and
hastening, hope for their Lord, often depressed but also full of hu-
mor. It conceals a joy that is not owned but granted afresh each day,
based on the great Yes that is Jesus Christ, without which human
reality could not be sustained.

From 1915, Barth studied with great zeal the works of the
Blumhardts, with their message of the kingdom of God that bursts
through all human barriers and takes the side of the socially
wronged and oppressed—the kingdom whose reality is summed up
in the affirmation: "Jesus is Victor." Barth's passiontide address of
1917 gives evidence of the influence of the Blumhardts.

Ah yes, "reality"; usually a good and well-filled hour that
runs as it should, tasks, cares, work, pleasures, growing
older, gaining experience, quarreling, making up again, interests jealously guarded against others, rights that no one
must touch, sometimes a great mistake and fall, sometimes a
good impulse and act, and now and then, amid all this, some
thought of God or the destiny that so strangely integrates and
directs everything. Then suddenly, of course, the shocking
sign of something quite different and unexpected, for example, murderers and rascals who surprise and irritate us, fami-

lies which for all their outward decorum are inwardly poisoned by a remarkable bitterness, sicknesses that prowl around like wild beasts seeking their prey, the crying needs of the poor, perhaps at our very gates without our knowing it, a war that breaks out and lasts some three years, and no one can ask why, because we all know only too well. These things arise like ghosts and interrupt the hour for a moment and then disappear again. And death from time to time puts the sudden, final question: What now? Yes, these things are all present along with life's normal course; they are part of the world as it is. And behind it all there is ultimately a feeling that perhaps things are not really for the best, that something might be basically awry. There is an unrest and sadness for which there is no special reason, a certain sighing: Yes, life is hard, and people are strange, and there is much that we do not understand, and it is well to sleep it off and forget it. . . . But something else we do not grasp so well, namely, that Jesus did not stay on this side but crossed the frontier as Joshua once crossed the Jordan, or Blücher the Rhine in 1814, or the Germans the Belgian frontier a hundred years later. What was he seeking there? What good can come of it? What pain or disorder does it remove? Why does he not stay with his fine thoughts, with his great hopes and pure heart, with his "God," by the blue lake of Gennesaret or among the birds and flowers on the fields of Galilee? Everything seemed to go well there, but not in Jerusalem. Why was he not content to gather a little garland or gathering of children of God away from the clamor of the world? Why, why did he have to cross the frontier . . . ?

Into the humming clockwork of everyday life comes the call: All things shall be new. . . .

Into our sadness and unrest and graveyard mood comes the message: I live, and you shall live also. To all the puzzles and questions of life this is the only valid answer: God. And this means that we may be sure, and cling to it, that all the puzzles and questions and difficulties and cruelties of life can exist only behind God's back, and that they are there no longer when we see God face to face. To begin again with

God means seeing that we cannot go on as we are. To build again with God means that we cannot go running or creeping on in the old groove, in the old, bad, accustomed routine. It means looking to see if God's light and power are not visible, and they are often closer than we think. It means waiting . . . not in the void, but for God's redemption, for the bars of our prison to burst open suddenly. Jesus has summoned God's kingdom into real life as the surest and most real of all things. . . .

Look, this is the great frontier crossing of Jesus. This is the great movement of all who have really been or will be God's pilgrims. It means going with him if we seriously mean what we sing so gladly. Follow me, says Jesus our hero. All else we do may be fine and good and religious and Christian, but it is not following Jesus.

Über die Grenze, Zofingen (1917), pp. 6–10.

In May and June 1920, Barth was zealously studying 2 Corinthians, and he found Chapter 5 particularly full of insights and prospects. He preached on 5:1ff. on June 20, 1920, under the title "Confident Despair."

Paul twice says: "We groan." It does not matter whether the groaning is expressed or concealed. Most groaning is quiet and suppressed, known only to one person and God. For the most part, at any rate, it is an inner movement, an unrest and anxiety, a struggling for breath, that comes upon us when we are at the point of losing heart and are no longer able to prevent ourselves from doing so. Groaning is the final stage before despair. There reigns in it something of the great darkness of weak surrender to an unavoidable terror, to a fatal sinking into nothingness, to an acceptance of death. But the darkness is not yet total. There is still a longing for freedom, a questioning and complaining, a last looking for the distant light of life. I think we know these last stages before despair. We should not exaggerate when we are hard pressed and sad. We should not think that we are already in despair. Fortunately, this is not usually so. To reach this state is too terrible for us to think that even when things are going badly for us we have already reached it. But groaning, the last station before it, many of us know only too well, and all of us to some extent. . . .

Paul tells us something very remarkable in this text. He tells us that if we really know why we are groaning, we can do so with confidence. . . .

And now Paul makes a really big assertion. We must not repeat it too quickly; but we must make a reverent effort at least to hear it. He tells us that we groan and think we know why. But we do not really know. We are mistaken about ourselves. We must learn to understand ourselves. Yes, the meaning of what we call life is death. But the meaning of death is true life. . . .

There is a yes in you dying people who are shut up under the great no, a yes that is immeasurably higher and other than your whole existence, beyond comparison with every little earthly yes that you would like to have or attain, heavenly over against everything earthly and yet not alien, distant and yet not distant, your own most proper portion and inheritance, your home. We know that "we have a building from God, a house not made with hands, eternal in the heavens." This is why we groan. Do you see why we have to groan? Yes, the present tent must be pulled down so that the building from God may receive you. What makes you groan, however, is not that the tent must be pulled down but that the building from God has not yet received you. . . .

If there were no God, if the heavenly house did not await us, we would not need to groan. But God has set us in a movement, in unrest and anxiety. We have to groan because God is the cause of our groaning. . . .

If we can hear and understand that, we can perhaps hear and understand more. Because it is God, says Paul, who has brought it about that we must groan in this life, our groaning is not without confidence. With it we are very close to the bad outcome of despair. But we do not reach it. In truth, we are infinitely far from it. We will not lose courage; we cannot do so. God has encouraged us. When we know ourselves, when we see that God is the reason for our groaning, then we achieve an insight that gives us confidence in the greatest and deepest sadness. We see death in the light of life. We justify God, who by his Spirit causes us to groan in this tent. We see the necessity of death and of the no in transitoriness. They are needed to free a place. As they do their work, true life comes closer. We are closer to the goal of being clothed upon with our heavenly dwelling. . . .

Who among us knows this too? We barely know it, and hence we barely understand what Paul is saying. Even less do we understand that he was truly confident in this world in which we cannot be confident, that he did not become a desert hermit with these insights, that he did not shut himself up in a little room with a few believers, that he did not seek rest, but that with these insights he lived and fought and suffered and fell and rose again and rejoiced, filling the world, this world, the world of death and the no, with his deeds, setting it in motion to the glory of God. This confidence is beyond our horizon. We can see again at this point what Christ was for Paul, the crucified Christ. He testified that he saw in him the world's turning point, the breakthrough from the most terrible no to the most glorious yes, the ending of what is called life by death, and the manifestation of true life beyond death, the extinguishing of all lights and the rising of a great light out of darkness. Humanity without God, and then God coming to humanity, God with us—Immanuel. This gave Paul his insight. He saw why we groan. He saw the house built by God. He saw that the tent must be put off. He saw that he had to accept what had made him shudder most. He groaned and yet he was confident. He had seen the *resurrection*.

Komm Schöpfer Geist! Predigten, Munich (1932), pp. 246ff., 250, 253ff. (ET London [1978] cf. pp. 267ff., 275ff.).

On July 25, 1922, at the invitation of the General Superintendent,
D. Jacobi, Barth addressed the clergy of Saxony on "The Need and
Promise of Christian Preaching."

It always makes me a little self-conscious to hear such serious talk of "my theology." Not because I think that what I am doing is anything other or better than just theology. I think I have overcome the childish ailment of being ashamed of theology. Some of you know it perhaps, and have perhaps already overcome it. No, the real reason is that I have to ask myself with some perplexity what this theology of mine really is . . . that I am supposed to "introduce" to you in outline. I have cause to sigh about this often enough, but I have to admit frankly that all I can call my theology, if I see it correctly, amounts finally only to one point . . . not a standpoint but a mathematical point . . . a mere viewpoint. Everything else that belongs to a real theology with me is only in its opening stages, and I do not know whether I will ever get beyond these, or even wish to do so. . . .

I know that we cannot stand in the air, but willy-nilly have to have at least one foot on the earth. I know that I am not the first or only one to long for a pilgrim theology that would cut right across all existing theological possibilities, right, left, and center—understanding, embracing, and transcending them all. Who, today, does not want to be in some way above movements of the day? I also know that none of the real or supposed pilgrim theologians has ever finished his course . . . without erecting . . . at least a gypsy tent that was then treated . . . as a text instead of a gloss, as a new theology. . . .

It cannot be a matter of polemically establishing a new position or even a new negation. It must be a matter of reflecting on what is said and done, of reflecting on the one necessary and inescapable thing that our churches and we clergy confront more than ever today, of reflection that means recollection of the meaning of what we do and say. . . .

To groan "Come, Creator Spirit" is, according to Romans

8, more hopeful than to triumph as if we already had him. You are already introduced to "my theology" if you have heard this groan. If you have heard and understood this, . . . then you will also understand if I close with a confession of hope. Commenting on Micah 4:6, Calvin said that the church is sometimes hardly distinguishable from a dead or sick person. Nevertheless, we need not despair. For the Lord raises up his own just as he awakened the dead from the grave. We should note this. For when the church does not shine, we think too quickly that it is extinguished and done for. But the church is so upheld in the world that it will suddenly rise from the dead. . . . Let us cling to the fact that the church is not without resurrection, and more than that, not without many resurrections.

Das Wort Gottes und die Theologie, Munich (1924), pp. 99ff., 122ff. (ET New York [1957], cf. pp. 97ff., 134ff.).

Lecturing in Hungary in 1936, Barth answered the question of what we should do if we cannot pray.

Let me first ask: Who *can* pray? Is there any one of us who can say, I can pray? I am afraid that if someone did, it would not really be true. Conversely, those who complain, I cannot pray, are told: Precisely thus are you close to real praying. Real prayer is something *we* cannot do. It is something that happens. It happens through us, yet not on the basis of any ability of ours, but on the basis of the fact that God has accepted us as his children. If we are his children, then we cry to him. The acceptance and the consequent crying are beyond our capacity. We cannot do them. But the command of the Bible bids us pray. And you perhaps stand there and can only repeat the complaint: I cannot. Keep before your eyes our Lord Jesus Christ, who prayed on the cross for us. Then you can only accept his grace. But if you say yes to his grace, then you obey his command, you pray. The little sigh with which we say to God, "Ah yes," is prayer and the source of all prayer. It contains the whole of the Lord's Prayer, and every *Miserere* and *Gloria* the church has ever prayed. This little sigh contains it all, and it all comes back again to this little sigh. There is no art in prayer, only the simple fact that God's children may pray. Making use of this "may" is what you should do when you cannot pray.

Theologische Existenz heute 47, Munich (1936), p. 56 ("Gottes Gnadenwahl").

On October 3, 1947, Barth preached in Basel on Psalm 3. He included the sermon in a volume that he entitled "Fear not" because we need have no other fear if, loving God above all things, we fear him above all things (CD II, 1, pp. 32f.; I, 2, p. 646).

David does not look at himself, neither at the abysses of his life, his sin and the severity of God's punishment, nor at the high points of his life, his great work and deeds, the fine aspects of life and character that he certainly did not lack. Looking neither at the former nor the latter, David looks only at the one thing that is above him, beyond his sin and beyond his uprightness. He looks at God's promise, which his sin obscures but does not take away. He did not repel grace by sinning, and hence he may and must stand as we see him here: confident, cheerful, and victorious, he the great sinner. What can we do that great sinners such as we all are may stand like that? Dear friends, we can do nothing. Only Jesus Christ and the Holy Spirit can do it in grace. David does not speak here. God speaks through David. He speaks through David to us. May this be our prayer in this hour!

"O Lord, how many are my foes! Many are rising against me; many are saying of me, there is no help for him in God." Look, this great sinner is attacked but not defeated. Attacked indeed! David has many enemies, people who do not know God's covenant with him, or do not want to know it. There are many, he says, who want to take away the king-

dom and promise from him. And God has let these people attack him. His sin makes the plight he finds himself in unavoidable. This attack from his enemies is in God's name. He
will find no help in God, they charge. What reply can he
give? Are they not in the right, ten times, a thousand times
in the right against him? There is no help for him, the great
sinner, in God. His whole situation and his own conscience
seem to tell him that this is truly so. He is attacked, yet not
defeated—no, not defeated.

Listen to his cry: "O Lord." His whole complaint lies in
this "O Lord." My friends, so long as this "O Lord" rises up
from our hearts and lips, all is well with us. Many foes may
be against us. They may be ten times or a thousand times in
the right against us. But we survive their attack. They will not
destroy God's covenant with us.

Fürchte dich nicht!, Munich (1949), pp. 137f.

*On May 24, 1942 (Pentecost), Barth preached on Ephesians 1:8 in
St. Jakob, Basel.*

We cannot possibly justify ourselves if we really want to
be different from that first community at Pentecost. We cannot be other than that gathering, or elsewhere than in it. Is
it not incomparably glorious that we cannot be elsewhere,
that there is no reason in heaven or earth for us to be
different?

But perhaps you ask how it is we think we see that we
can unfortunately be different. What then? The only thing
then is that we must and will begin to pray, and not cease to
pray, and to ask that we be rescued from the evil bewitchment (for that is what it is) and the evil stupidity (for that is
what it is) of which we are guilty. That the blinkers be taken
from our eyes and the wax from our ears. That like little children learning their first steps, we should learn to accept the
fact, and stick to it, that God's grace has flowed over

us. . . . If we pray, if we do so merely with the sigh and cry, "Father," then we can count on it that the darkness, bewitchment, and stupidity will give place. That little sigh, as Luther once wrote, will pierce the clouds and fill heaven and earth, and the angels will think they never heard any sound like it, and God himself will hear nothing else in the whole world, for it is Jesus Christ himself in us — almighty, reigning, victorious. In spite of every weakness, temptation, and assault, we are surely in the community of those who know and rejoice with thanksgiving that God's grace has flowed over us.

Fürchte dich nicht!, Munich (1949), pp. 245f.

On December 26, 1959, Barth wrote an article on "The Great Yes" in a Bern weekly. He had often preached on similar themes, for example: "The Great But" on February 27, 1921 (Prov. 16:2).

Yes means agreement, acceptance. I had a little grandson . . . whose first and only German word for a long time was the little word yes . . . a distinctively intensive and friendly yes. The possibility that he might also say no seemed to be unknown to him. He obviously accepted what he saw and heard around him. It still gladdens and comforts me when I think of it, because it is a distant recollection of the great Yes.

The great Yes, unlike that of the youngster, contains a clear No in it, not alongside it, but in it. No means rejection; it implies that something is wrong, perverted, bad. The great Yes contains a No like that. There is no sharper No. When the great Yes sounds forth and is heard, it exposes the arrogance, stupidity, deception, and self-deception of the world and people. It condemns and judges, banishing all complacency and conceit, for the great Yes does not let us justify ourselves or boast. If we think we are good and upright, this is a sure sign that we have not heard the great Yes.

The great Yes is a Nevertheless. Yes, world, yes, human-

ity, yes, you are dear to me, yes, I accept you, even though
you do not in the least deserve it, even though I have every
reason for the opposite. I say yes to you when I have good
reason to say no. I oppose to this good reason the better reason of my glorious, righteous, and holy Nevertheless, the
Nevertheless of grace. In this Nevertheless I say yes to you.
Hear the No so that I may tell you that I say yes. You will not
hear me unless you will hear the No concealed in my Yes.

The great Yes is a Therefore. Yes, world, yes, humanity,
you are dear to me, I accept you in spite of everything, because first and last I have mercy on you. I have mercy on you
because I am always faithful to you. I am always faithful to
you because I remember that I was your Creator and will be
your Redeemer and Consummator. This basis of my Yes—my
mercy, faithfulness, and recollection—is deeper and stronger
than the deepest and strongest basis I have for saying no to
you. For this reason I oppose to my No my glorious, righteous, and holy Nevertheless. For this reason I chide, but in
the wrath of the great love in which I seek you. I say no, but
the No sounds forth and is heard, not alongside my Yes, but
only included, enclosed, and concealed within it.

The great Yes is a Whither: it has a definite purpose and
goal. Yes, world, yes, humanity, I have mercy on you, and
am faithful, and remember my kindness as Creator and
Redeemer; I do so in spite of every reason to deal with you
differently, in order to save you from your perversion, in order to transform you into a new world and a new humanity.
This will of mine makes my sentence and verdict, and therefore my No, unavoidable. But in this good will my No can
only be included in my Yes. Because of my good will, my No
cannot be my first or last word. It cannot be spoken and
heard alongside the word of my grace, contradicting it. It can
only show that my grace is real, free grace. My will is to enlighten and help and save you. What but my supreme Yes
can do this?

We are speaking about God's *Yes*. . . . No human heart
has conceived it (1 Cor. 2:9). Of ourselves, none of us can say
this great Yes to the world or to ourselves or to our fellows.

But God has said it and does say it. As his word of grace, it has come down to us. It is the great Yes of Christmas, Good Friday, Easter, Pentecost. Jesus Christ is the great Yes. In Jesus Christ God's No to the world and humanity, his sentence and judgment, is frightfully visible, but it is enclosed in his mercy, faithfulness, and recollection of his goodness; it is caught up in his good will to enlighten, help, and save us. In Jesus Christ, God unequivocally accepts us; we are unequivocally righteous before him. As Paul says, "The Son of God, Jesus Christ . . . was not Yes and No, but in him it is always Yes. For all the promises of God find their Yes in him. That is why we utter the Amen through him, to the glory of God" (2 Cor. 1:19–20). . . .

Against the great Yes that is Jesus Christ there can be no scruple, doubt, or objection. In the truth and power of this great Yes every No . . . becomes a little no. In this great Yes the world and all of us are sheltered in the battle none of us is spared, and we are empowered to offer stout resistance to sin, death, and the devil. This great Yes carries an irresistible summons to all of us to advance (to the freedom of the children of God, cf. Rom. 8:21). By this great Yes, and by it alone, we may live with maturity and soberness.

If I might close with a certain Advent sigh, it can only be this: Oh, if only the voice of the church in the world (its theology, preaching, and practical word to itself and others) were much, much more the voice of witnesses to the one necessary thing (Lk. 10:42), the great Yes that encloses but also overcomes what in it has become every little No.

Predigten 1954–1967, Zurich (1981), 267-270.

Epilogue

I HAVE NO SERIOUS COMPLAINT against anyone or anything apart from my own failure today, yesterday, the day before, and the day before that—I mean my failure to be truly grateful. Perhaps I still have some difficult days ahead, and sooner or later I have the day of my death. What remains for me is that in relation to yesterday and all the days that preceded it, and all those that may follow it, and finally the last day that will surely come, I should constantly hold up before me and impress upon myself: "Forget not all his benefits" (Ps. 103:2).

Briefe 1961-1968, Zurich (1979), p. 480 (ET Grand Rapids [1981], p. 298).

I am sometimes frightened when I see the amount of free and unmerited grace that has ruled over and in my life, action, and work. It has been almost like something alien, in strange contrast to my own life day by day and year by year, in which I . . . have rather wheezily thought and spoken and written what seemed to follow next, although always under the impression that I was some distance behind what was really happening. I have always had in mind the many who have worked just as hard as I have, or harder, but whose days, unlike mine, have been lived out in obscurity or semi-obscurity. To be "famous" ("the greatest scholar of our time," as I even read as icing on the cake) is all very pleasant. But who will finally be praised? I beg you, then, to continue your kindness to me and to accompany me with your thoughts and encouragements. I also admonish you in all seriousness, don't make a myth out of me, for the angels will certainly not

111

like that, and the perspicacious will see through it to my
shame. Let each try to do what I have attempted, doing in his
own field, better than I have done, a little something that will
be to the glory of God and his neighbors.

Briefe 1961–1968, Zurich (1979), p. 2 (ET Grand Rapids [1981], pp. 3f.).

Theology, however, demands free people. As a young
theologian, I belonged to a school. It was not a bad school.
I still think of my teachers of that time with gratitude. But
later I had to free myself from their school, not because much
in their teaching was wrong, but simply because it was a
school. I do not want the result of my life to be the formation
of a new school. I want to tell everyone here who will listen
that I myself am not a "Barthian," for when I have learned
anything, I have wanted to remain free to learn more. Understand what I say: Make as little use of my name as possible.
There is only one relevant name, and exalting others can only
lead to false ties and provoke irksome jealousy and stubborn-
ness in others. Do not take any statement from me untested,
but measure all of them by the one true Word of God, who
is the judge and supreme teacher of us all. You get me right
if you let yourselves be led by what I say to what *he* says.
Good theologians do not live in houses of ideas, principles,
and methods. They pass through every house and out again
into the free world. They keep on the move. They have before
them the high and distant mountains and the unending
ocean of God—and also, in close proximity, their fellows,
good and bad, fortunate and unfortunate, Christian and pa-
gan, Western and Eastern, to whom in all modesty they may
be witnesses.

Offene Briefe 1945–1968, Zurich (1984), p. 375.

If it ever comes to light who has been the greatest theologian of this century, then perhaps some little man or
woman who has very quietly taught a Bible class somewhere
will be discovered and will actally prove to have been the
greatest theologian of this century. At least to the extent that

"greatest" and "theologian" may be combined. In my last larger work, the *Introduction to Evangelical Theology*, I expressly stated that there might have been great anatomists . . . or musicians . . . but great theologians is strictly a contradiction in terms. As theologians, we can never be great, but at best we can only be small in our own way. The whole idea is impossible.

Evangelische Theologie 26, Munich (1966), p. 617.

It is undoubtedly good when people faithfully accomplish some big or little thing in their lives. Why should they not be glad about it? I myself know someone who has been fairly industrious, has written books, some of them bulky, has taught students, has often been in the papers, and even finally in the *Spiegel*. So what! But finally, why not? Just one thing is certain: We all have our time (Eccl. 3:1), no more. One day others will come who will do the same things better. . . . And one thing is even more certain: Whether our achievement be great or small, significant or insignificant, we shall all stand before our eternal Judge, and all that we have done and achieved will be no more than a molehill.

Predigten 1954–1967, Zurich (1981), p. 160.

I have indeed become so free as to be able to write dogmatics — which many notable theologians are afraid of doing. Most theologians, especially today, write only little pamphlets and articles and Festschrift contributions. I was never content with this. I said to myself: "If I am a theologian, I must try to work out broadly what I think I have perceived as God's revelation. What I think *I* have perceived. Yet not I as an individual but I as a member of the Christian church." This is why I call my book *Church Dogmatics*. "Church" here does not mean that the church is responsible for all that I say, but that I as one member of the church have reflected on what may be perceived in revelation and tried to present it to the best of my conscience and understanding.

Letzte Zeugnisse, Zurich (1970), p. 38 (ET Grand Rapids [1977], p. 36).

The last word I have to say . . . is not a concept like grace but a name: Jesus Christ. He is grace and he is the ultimate one beyond world and church and even theology. We cannot lay hold of him. But we have to do with him. And my own concern in my long life has been increasingly to emphasize this name and to say, "In him." There is no salvation but in this name. In him is grace. In him is the spur to work, warfare, and fellowship. In him is all that I have attempted in my life in weakness and folly. It is there in him.

Letzte Zeugnisse, Zurich (1970), pp. 30f. (ET Grand Rapids [1977], pp. 29f.).

Karl Barth Chronology

1886 (May 10) Born in Basel
1889 Family moved to Bern
1901–1902 Confirmation classes under Robert Aeschbacher
1904–1908 Studies in Bern, Berlin, Tübingen, Marburg
1908 Assistant Editor of *The Christian World*
1909–1911 Assistant Pastor in Geneva
1911–1921 Pastor in Safenwil
1912 Death of Fritz Barth, Barth's father
1912 Marriage to Nelly Hoffmann (d. 1976) Children: Franziska, b. 1914; Markus, b. 1915; Christoph, b. 1917; Matthias, b. 1919–d. 1941; Hans Jakob, b. 1925–d. 1984
1915 Joined Swiss Social Democratic Party
1919 *Romans* (1st edition)
1921–1925 Professor in Göttingen
1922 *Romans* (2nd edition)
1922–1933 *Zwischen den Zeiten*
1925–1930 Professor at Münster
1930–1935 Professor at Bonn
1931 Joined German Social Democratic Party
1932ff. *Church Dogmatics*
1933 *Theologische Existenz heute*
1934 (May 31) Barmen Declaration
1935 Forced retirement from Bonn
1935–1962 Professor at Basel
1938 Death of Anna Barth, Barth's mother
1940ff. Military Service (Auxiliary)
1946–1947 Guest Lectures in Bonn

1952   British Award "For Service in the Cause of Freedom"
1954–1964   Sermons in Basel Prison
1956   Tribute to Mozart
1961–1962   *Evangelical Theology* (Last Lectures at Basel)
1962   Visit to USA
1963   Sonning Prize (Copenhagen)
1966   Rome Visit
1966–1968   Final Seminars at Basel
1968   Sigmund Freud Prize
1968   (December 10) Death

English Translations of Barth's Works

* *The Christian Life*, Eerdmans (1981)
  Come Holy Spirit, Mowbray (1978)
* *Church Dogmatics*, T. and T. Clark: I,1 (1975); I,2 (1956); III,3 (1960); III,4 (1961); IV,2 (1958); IV,3 (1962)
  Epistle to the Romans, Oxford (1935)
* *Evangelical Theology*, Eerdmans (1981)
* *Final Testimonies*, Eerdmans (1977)
  The Knowledge of God and the Service of God, Hodder (1938)
* *A Late Friendship*, Eerdmans (1982)
* *Letters 1961–1968*, Eerdmans (1981)
  W. A. Mozart, Harper and Row (1959); reprinted, Eerdmans (1986)
  Protestant Theology in the Nineteeth Century, Judson (1972)
  Theological Existence Today, Hodder (1933); reprinted 1962 (Lexington, Kentucky)
  The Word of God and the Word of Man, Harper (1957)

* Denotes translations followed in the present text.